MAGNUS FIN
AND THE
MOONLIGHT MISSION

MAGNUS FIN
AND THE FIN
MOONLIGHT MISSION

JANIS MACKAY

 Kelpies

Kelpies is an imprint of Floris Books

First published in 2011 by Floris Books

© 2011 Janis Mackay

Janis Mackay has asserted her right under the
Copyright, Designs and Patents Act 1988
to be identified as the Author of this Work.

All rights reserved. No part of this book may be
reproduced without the prior permission of
Floris Books, 15 Harrison Gardens, Edinburgh
www.florisbooks.co.uk

The publisher acknowledges subsidy from
Creative Scotland towards the publication
of this series.

Mixed Sources
Product group from well-managed
forests and other controlled sources
www.fsc.org Cert no. TT-COC-2139
© 1996 Forest Stewardship Council

British Library CIP Data available
ISBN 978-086315-796-7
Printed by CPI Cox and Wyman, Reading, RG1 8EX

I dedicate this book to my dad,
Alexander Ramsay Mackay

Chapter 1

Magnus Fin ran along the shore path in the grey dawn light. He cut down to the sandy beach, kicking up tangles of seaweed as he ran. Feeling like King of the Sea and Shore, Magnus Fin let out a good loud whoop. An oystercatcher down at the water's edge whooped back.

Being alone at the beach in the early morning was always special, but low-tide mornings like this were even more so. Low tide meant secret rock pools, each like a miniature ocean. It meant more stones to scramble over. And it meant he'd be able to see the top of the mast of the sunken ship.

In a flash Magnus Fin was down on the skerries, the sloping black rocks that went out to sea. They spent half their lives hidden underwater. Now here they were, craggy, slippery and full of surprises. Fin leapt over stones and slithered on seaweed. He hoisted himself up his favourite rock, the high black one that jutted above all the others. Fin's feet knew its ledges and craggy footholds. Panting hard, he reached the top and stood tall, just in time to see the beaming orange sun burst over the sea's horizon. What an entrance! Up and up it rose, like King Midas, turning everything to gold.

Magnus Fin whipped out his penny whistle. He could only play one tune but he played it well and he played it twice.

And sure enough, up they came, their sleek round heads lifting out of the shining water. A wide smile burst over the boy's face. Quickly he counted: sixteen, seventeen, eighteen seals, and every one of them watching him. There were black ones, mottled grey ones, small silver calves and huge long-whiskered bulls.

Fin pocketed his whistle, took a deep breath, cupped his hands round his mouth then shouted, "HELLO, SEALS!"

He waited for the reply. And it came: shy at first then lifting into a rousing choir – the seal's song. Yelping, honking, soft for a moment then soaring. Like a trumpet, a bass guitar, bagpipes! What a sound!

When their song ended Magnus Fin clapped loudly, and the seals, lifting their flippers and splashing them together with yelping cries, clapped too. One by one they kicked out their tail fins, then, with a loud gurgling plunge, flipped under the water and vanished. Behind them the thin mast of the sunken ship remained, like a finger, pointing to the sky.

By this time the sun was up and the chill of the November dawn was gone. Glancing behind him Magnus Fin saw how everything was on fire. The golden sand on the beach shone. The hillsides and the cliff faces all glowed, meaning (because he could read time by the sun) that it was quarter past eight. That gave him half an hour to scramble about on the skerries, study the rock pools then comb the beach before a quick breakfast, then school.

In his bedroom Magnus Fin had a growing collection of pottery bits. He planned to make a mosaic picture, once he'd found a few more pieces of broken plates and coloured glass. The tideline was the best place to find broken pottery. Blue bits, that's what he wanted.

He bent his knees and swung his arms back, ready to jump from his high rock – when something by his feet caught his eye. He dropped his arms and stared. To the side of his right foot he saw a strange white mark. *Gull droppings?* He peered closer. It didn't look like gull droppings. He got down on his knees to examine it.

The mark looked like writing. It hadn't been there the day before; he was sure about that. This was his rock, his lookout tower. Being high up, this rock let him see, close-up, what the black-backed gulls were up to, puffins even if he was lucky, or gannets, diving at sixty miles an hour into the sea, or, most importantly, the seals. So what was this mysterious white mark doing on his rock?

Forgetting his plan to search for pottery, Fin stared at what appeared to be silvery writing. He let his finger follow its trail. It looked and felt like the letter M. Fin pulled his finger back and a shiver ran down his spine.

He glanced over his shoulder to the sea. The seals had gone. Normally they stayed close by, tumbling over in the water, or simply staring at him with their large kind eyes. Where were they? Fin scanned the beach. Not even a dog walker was out this early.

"You're brave now, remember that," he said to himself, standing up straight. "And it's only a silly mark on the stone. A rusty nail on a piece of driftwood, tossed on a high wave could have made that mark." Magnus Fin looked around for driftwood but, save for a tangle of seaweed and a plastic bottle, nothing else had been brought in by the tide.

He peered out over the bay. It was a crinkly kind of sea and, apart from the swishing sound of the waves breaking over the skerries, it was quiet. Most of the sea birds had flown south for the winter. Only the oystercatchers patrolling the shoreline and a few gulls bobbing on the waves remained. And they couldn't write the letter M on his rock, could they?

He tried to shake off the mood. He bent down and rubbed his hand over the M to erase it, but the harder he rubbed the stronger it became.

"Don't be daft, Fin – it's nothing," he said to himself out loud. Then he said it again, even louder, "Nothing at all!" Shouting like that made him feel braver. Magnus Fin jumped down, landing on a shelf of rock below. Now his heart really did thump wildly. Scrawled upon the ledge of this rock the letter F stared up at him. M F.

He bent closer. And – jeepers creepers – there were more. Loads of tiny scrawled initials. The rock was shouting with Ms and Fs! Fin felt his knees turn to jelly.

Someone, or something, was trying to contact him. His heart skipped a beat. Frantically he looked around, but the beach was empty. Who would write his initials on the rocks? Tarkin?

Forgetting about beachcombing, magic pools and mosaics, Fin scrambled over the rocks then raced across the sandy beach and up to the grassy path that led home. Tarkin liked unusual kinds of jokes. Trust his best friend to do something offbeat like rock writing.

"Find anything on the beach this morning?" Fin's mother asked.

Magnus Fin shook his head.

His mother sipped her tea. "Well, did you see the seals?"

Fin nodded.

"And did the tide take your tongue away by any chance?" she asked, ruffling his mop of black hair. "Go on now. Eat your toast, son. You know how important breakfast is."

He knew, but the strange marks on the rocks had done something to his appetite, and his tongue.

When Magnus Fin reached the school gates, early for once and out of breath, he looked down the hill to the sea below. It was strange to think of his initials down there on the rocks at the water's edge. *That'll be Tarkin playing a joke*, Fin thought, hoping so. Magnus Fin was still getting used to having a friend. There was a lot that Magnus Fin was getting used to.

Since turning eleven back in the summer his life had changed completely. Until then Magnus Fin had believed he was like everyone else, just lonelier. It was on his eleventh birthday that his father had told him the truth: that he was the son of a selkie father and a human mother. That's why he had different coloured eyes: his green eye was for the water and his brown eye for the earth. That was also the reason for his webbed feet, though most of the time he kept them well hidden.

"You are *Sliochan Nan Ron*," his father Ragnor had said, but Fin had shaken his head, not understanding. "Related to the seal folk," Ragnor had said with pride. "You're one of us." That was five months ago. A lot had happened since then, like finding a best friend.

Tarkin, originally from the United States, turned up in June, with his ponytail, shark's tooth necklace and enthusiasm for all things weird and adventurous. Tarkin's mother had taken him halfway round the world looking for "the perfect home", leaving Tarkin's dad behind in the Yukon in Canada.

Fin's loneliness ended the day Tarkin arrived and now, pushing the school gate open, Fin thought, maybe that's what best friends do. Best friends write to you – in unusual places! Don't they?

Chapter 2

"You, boy, tell the rest of P7 what five per cent of six pounds is." Mr Sargent's voice boomed across the classroom, breaking in on a vision of the letters M and F blazoned across enormous rocks.

Magnus Fin blinked and the vision disappeared. His heart thudded beneath his ribs for the umpteenth time that morning. It thudded, not because he didn't know what five per cent of six pounds was. He did. Tarkin, quick as lightning, had traced the number on his desk with his finger. It thudded because he hated Mr Sargent calling him "you, boy". He was always doing it, and every time Magnus Fin bit his lip and said nothing. This time, though, he only had two choices: burst into tears or blurt out how he felt. The writing on the rocks had shaken him up and before he knew it out tumbled the words, "My name is Magnus Fin."

"Excuse me?"

"I said – Magnus Fin. That's my name."

Everyone stared at the skinny boy with the mop of black hair and the strange mismatched eyes. Nobody spoke back to Mr Sargent, least of all shy little Magnus Fin.

The teacher's face turned red. His moustache twitched. The veins on his neck pulsed as if they might explode any second. But Magnus Fin had started so he kept going.

"I mean – everybody else gets called by their name – except me."

Tarkin was beaming at his friend in admiration. He made a thumbs-up gesture, winked then piped up, "I agree totally," which was a bad idea.

"It's not for you or anyone else to offer your opinion, *totally* or otherwise," shouted Mr Sargent, glaring now at Tarkin, who was twisting his long ponytail round his finger and chewing the end of it. "Break-time detention!"

Tarkin pulled a hair out of his mouth then shrugged his shoulders.

"And stop shrugging your shoulders. And stop eating your hair. And stop giving him, I mean Magnus, answers to questions."

"Magnus Fin," Tarkin said, then quickly added, "sir."

Mr Sargent could have gone either way. His nostrils flared. His shoulders rose up and his neck sank down. His huge fists clenched. A hissing noise came from his mouth. The whole class stared and held their breath. Then the teacher sighed loudly, sat down, shook his head and counted with great effort up to ten. When he had finished he stood up and looked at Magnus Fin.

"Yes, a name is important. Of course it is. Then tell me, Magnus Fin, what *is* five per cent of six pounds?"

"Um … thirty pence?"

So it was lunchtime before Fin could tell Tarkin what was bothering him. They were in the games hall because it had started to rain, on the climbing frame, right at the top.

"Don't look down, Tarkin, but something's up."

"Like?" said Tarkin slowly, his cheek pressed against the side of the bar.

"Like – I have to know – was it you?"

"Did what?"

"Who wrote M F on the rocks."

Magnus Fin could tell by the baffled look on his friend's face that it wasn't. He groaned. "Well, I think someone or something's trying to, um, write to me."

"OK? Like who, Fin? Where? When?"

"On my rock. I saw it this morning. Something's up under the sea, I just know it."

Magnus Fin shifted his leg and for a scary second his foot dangled high in midair before it found the steel bar. He glanced down. "Wow!" he gasped.

"Don't look down, Fin. Hey, could be they need you under the sea. You know? Your family down there. Hey, maybe I can go too? Cool!"

Fin lifted his chin and forced himself not to look down at the other pupils, playing dodgeball down below. "Come on, Tarkin, we'd better get down." Slowly they climbed down the frame, feet feeling for the bars and hands clutching on for dear life. "It gives me the creeps," said Magnus Fin.

"It's OK. We're almost down." Tarkin clutched the steel bar. "Whatever you do, man, just don't think about falling."

But it wasn't falling off the climbing frame that gave Magnus Fin the creeps. It was the letters on the rocks. He couldn't get them out of his mind.

When he closed his eyes they were there, like neon lights, flashing.

When he opened his mouth to speak there they were on his tongue: "Must fly! Many fish! Mad fiend! Much fun!"

"What are you going on about now, Magnus Fin?" boomed Mr Sargent.

"Oh! Um? Nothing, Mr Fargent – I mean Sargent, um, nothing!"

The other boys at school gave him the weird look, raised their eyebrows and twisted their fingers to their heads. Fin knew what that meant. Having one green eye and one brown eye, he was used to other children calling him crazy.

Maybe he was crazy? Maybe he'd just imagined the whole thing? Or maybe the rain had washed the letters away, or the tide? He wanted to check after school but he and Tarkin had joined the basketball club and today was basketball day.

"Catch, Fin," shouted Tarkin.

Fin caught it. He dribbled up the court. He dodged past Saul, then Emma, then Jamie-Lee. No one could stop him.

"Over here, Fin!" shouted Tarkin, who was now under the net, ready with his arms out. "Pass it here, Fin. Quick!"

Fin passed the ball and Tarkin caught it. But Pinky was right there, looming over Tarkin and defending the net. Pinky was tall and the school's best basketball player. He waved his arms in Tarkin's face, but Tarkin kept possession of the ball, then he jumped high, even higher than Pinky – and he scored!

So it was high fives all round, then oranges to suck on, then, all the way home, in the dark, it was the story of the incredible goal, the goal that won the match – again and again and again.

"You were fab, Fin, the way you dribbled up that court. I've never seen anyone dribble that fast. You should have seen Emma's face. Awesome, man, you could play for the Harlem Globetrotters any day."

"You jumped so high your head practically touched the net!"

"Not as cool as you standing up to Sargent Major though!" Tarkin gave Fin a friendly thump on the back.

The street lamps were on along the road to the harbour, making orange pools of light in the darkness. The two boys slowed down as they approached the bridge over the river. This was where they parted. Magnus Fin lived in an old fisherman's cottage on the other side of the river, close to the sea, at the end of an unlit track. He had no neighbours except for the beach, the brae and the sea. Tarkin lived at the other end of the village on a croft.

"Well, see ya, Fin," Tarkin said, swinging his rucksack in the air, still buzzing with the basketball victory.

"Yeah, see you." But as Fin turned to walk alone over the dark bridge the basketball buzz suddenly left him, like bathwater drains away down the plughole. He shivered. Swinging round he called out, "Tarkin?"

"Uh-huh?"

"Do you want to hear the seals singing tomorrow?"

"Cool."

"And maybe we could see if that writing on the rocks is still there?" Fin blurted out.

"Sure thing. I'll be there. What time?"

"Eight o'clock – down at the beach."

Tarkin grinned and stuck his thumbs up, then he turned round, skipped high in the air and ran along the road.

Magnus Fin listened to Tarkin's steps growing fainter until he couldn't hear them any more. Then he turned and headed over the bridge. After the afternoon's rain, the river was in spate and it gushed noisily under him.

Walking up the dirt track he counted the hours till eight o'clock the next morning. Fourteen – an eternity. Then he counted the minutes, or tried to. But by this time he could smell the tang of the sea and the smoke from their log fire. Then it wasn't long before the sweet smell of apple crumble reached him. Magnus Fin sprinted the rest of the way home.

Basketball, and climbing – to say nothing of all that worrying. He was starving!

Chapter 3

Aquella was doing her homework when Fin came home. Aquella was always doing homework. Magnus Fin's selkie cousin had come ashore five months earlier, so she was still getting used to being a land girl. Although the cottage was small, Fin's parents had managed to make her a bedroom in the attic with a window to the sea. Fin had helped her decorate it with shells and driftwood and brightly coloured scarves. The tattered blue dress she had worn when she first came ashore had been turned into a cushion.

After a delicious tea of fish, chips and apple crumble, Fin asked Aquella if she wanted to see his brand new beachcombing treasures: a kittiwake's skull and a pheasant's tail feather.

"OK, but then I have to practise sums or else I'll be in primary school for ever."

"What creatures under the sea can write?" Magnus Fin asked his cousin, as soon as they were both propped up on his boat-like bed.

"None as far as I know," she said, staring up at the brown fishing net that hung above Magnus Fin's bed. Aquella frowned. She liked her cousin's room, which they called Neptune's Cave. She loved the shells and driftwood, his shark posters and his treasure collection.

But she didn't like the net.

Fin nudged her. "But what about selkies when they're in their human skin? Can they write? Think hard, Aquella, it's really important."

Aquella thought hard. She brought strands of her long black hair up to her nose and smelt it.

"Well?"

"Mostly we danced. That's what I remember." Her green eyes shone with the memory. "And we stared at humans sometimes because we were fascinated by them. We hid behind rocks and watched people and sometimes we ran up into fields for fun and picked flowers." She laughed, her voice like a bubbling waterfall. "Sometimes we played tricks on people. We'd throw shells or pebbles into the water and make funny noises, then the humans would get frightened and run away. The best thing was if music was playing somewhere, then we'd hide and listen to it. But writing? I've never heard of that before. If I already knew how to read and write, school would be much easier."

Fin pulled a face and scratched his chin.

"Why, Fin?" she went on, prodding his arm. "Who wrote to you?"

"Something under the sea. Or someone. I mean – I think so."

They both fell silent then and thought about Miranda, their grandmother. Where was she now? A look of sadness fell across Aquella's face, fearing her selkie family might be in danger. And like the selkies Aquella and Fin were, they didn't have to put their thoughts into words. Thoughts travelled through water and air between them, like waves.

20

So if you're being called under the sea, Fin, you'd better go.

I know, Aquella.

And you don't have to wait for a full moon. Not now.

Magnus Fin stared at Aquella, his eyebrows knitting, confused.

The first time you entered our world, you needed the power of the moon. But this will be your second time, Fin. You're half selkie, half human. You always will be. Sliochan Nan Ron, *that's you. Now all you need is a low tide and a brave heart. You can go anytime – lucky you!*

It was hard for Aquella, not that she ever complained. Her seal skin had been destroyed by a wicked sea monster, and she was going through the transformation of becoming a land girl. To be able to survive on land, she had to avoid salt water for a year and a day.

Smiling, she reached over and gave Fin a friendly punch on the leg. *And tell them I'm fine here. Tell them it's good to be a girl.*

I will, if I find them.

And tell them school is fun.

He looked at her quizzically. She wiggled her nose then stuck out her tongue. Magnus grinned then pushed her off his bed and threw his pillow at her.

"Ouch!" She rubbed her elbow. "Good thing I've got my selkie fat to protect me."

Fin laughed. It was true; there was still a seal's roundness to Aquella. "So what's two plus two then, tubby?" he asked, flopping down onto his belly and pulling a face at her.

She pulled a face back, wedged as she now was between a lobster creel and a book about whales. "Twenty two?"

"Wrong."

She frowned then grabbed the pillow and threw it back at him – hard. "Take that you half-selkie!"

"And take that back, you selkie who can't even read. Or add up!"

"Ouch!" Aquella rubbed her shoulder where the pillow had hit her. But she was strong. She flung the pillow back, right at his head.

"Ow! That hurt!"

"And where's that kittiwake's skull anyway?" Aquella laughed. "And the feather? Bet you haven't even got one!" By this time she had grabbed Fin's other pillow. He held tight on to his own pillow, lifting it up like a shield.

"Have!"

Aquella stood up and whacked his pillow hard. "No you haven't!"

Then the two of them forgot about creatures under the sea and writing on rocks while the pillows exploded and white feathers flew up into the fishing net. Suddenly, in Neptune's Cave, in that cottage down by the sea, on a dark November's evening, it was snowing.

Chapter 4

Magnus Fin was down at the beach at half past seven the next morning. It was that grey time between night and day when the beach and the sea and the rocks look like an old photograph. The uneasy feeling of yesterday had gone and he felt excited. He couldn't imagine now why anyone would get upset about silly letters scratched on a rock. A pillow fight and a good night's sleep had done wonders. He ran across the beach, kicking up sand and scattering shells, feeling bravery surge through his muscles. He disturbed a lonely heron perched on a rock in the hillside. The wide-winged creature flew off with a dry cawing cry.

"Morning, Mr Heron," Fin called out, flinging his arms out to copy its slow-motion flight. The heron landed on a rock and hunched himself up, then stared down at the water.

Come on, Tark, Fin thought, looking around for his friend and hoping he'd come early. When the two of them were down at the beach together, skimming stones or messing about in rock pools, anything felt possible.

Magnus Fin ran across the beach towards the skerries. Maybe he'd do a spot of beachcombing and find some treasures while he waited. It had been a while since the tide had brought in anything really exciting. The old welly boot he'd found last week didn't count. The lobster creel didn't count either. Neither did the car tyre. They were everyday kinds of treasures. Rubbish, that's what his mum called them but Fin wasn't so sure. Sometimes amongst that rubbish you could find something really special – like a fork from the *Titanic*, or a silver heart necklace, a shark's tooth, or bits of blue pottery or glass.

He got down on his hands and knees and sifted through the sand for cowrie shells. They were supposed to bring good luck and he wanted to give Tarkin a present for sticking up for him yesterday. But cowrie shells, or "groatie buckies" as they were called in his village, were hard to come by. Fin found a piece of clear glass, with its sharp edges softened. This was sand glass, not blue but special all the same. Fin lifted it, brushed away the sand then peered through it.

The familiar scene around him was suddenly magnified. He saw glassy pink streaks in the sky and a fat glassy gull wheel in the air. Then he fixed his spyglass on the rocks in the distance and gulped. Something moved amongst the rocks, something bright yellow. He pulled the glass down and stared with wide eyes over the top of it. Someone in a bright yellow jacket was bending over the rock pools in the skerries. A winkle picker.

Winkle pickers always gave Magnus Fin a fright. Mostly he had the beach to himself. Even in the summer few tourists made it to this tucked-away stone and sand beach in the far north of Scotland. And most of the dog walkers in the village preferred to throw balls in the park.

Fin stayed where he was, down on his hands and knees in a patch of sand between stones, watching. He should have known. He'd noticed an old car parked up by the bridge. Winkle pickers worked at low tide and liked cold mornings. The colder the better, his father had told him. Maybe it was the winkle picker who had scratched his initials on the rocks?

Magnus Fin had stared at winkle pickers before, sometimes for a whole hour, and they rarely noticed him. They were so focused on finding periwinkles on the rocks, pulling them off and filling their buckets that they rarely looked around. Would the seals come up to sing if the winkle picker was on the skerries?

Just then a familiar voice called out in the distance, "Never fear – Tarkin's here!"

Fin glanced over his shoulder to see his friend galloping over the beach, whooping and yelling. Magnus Fin stood up, suddenly feeling much braver.

"Over here, Tark!" he shouted, waving him over.

The oystercatchers took off with shrill piercing cries and flew over the shallow water. Tarkin looked about him and whistled. "Hey! Brought your dad with you, Fin?"

"No. It's a winkle picker. He's pulling periwinkles off the rocks. You get eighty pounds for a bag of them."

"Wow! You ever tasted one?"

"Yeah, they're really salty."

Tarkin wrinkled his nose, pulled a face then seemed to forget the winkle picker. He jumped onto a grey rock and scanned the horizon. "There's the tip of the sun. Look! It's like a muckle basketball looming out of the sea. Cool!" Tarkin had been in Scotland five months now and learnt some Scottish words. Muckle was one of them, and he used it whenever he could.

The boys laughed then scrambled over the skerries. "Race you to the black rock!" Fin shouted. "Last one's a hairy kipper." They both slithered and slipped over the seaweed, shouting and laughing. Still the winkle picker ignored them.

Magnus Fin turned and shouted out, "Hello!"

The winkle picker lifted his head for a second, looked with pale blue piercing eyes at Fin then went back to his winkles. He had a straggly beard and a thin, weather-beaten face, but maybe no tongue in his head for he didn't return Fin's hello. While Magnus Fin stared at the winkle picker, Tarkin took his opportunity and scrambled on past him up to the high rock.

"Winner!" Tarkin shouted, lifting his long gangly arms high above his head. "So I guess you're the hairy kipper."

"That's not fair." Magnus Fin hauled himself up to stand beside his friend. "I would have won …"

"But you didn't. You lost focus. So, where are the seals?" Tarkin scanned the sea. The water was smooth. Nothing moved. Only far in the distance a fishing boat passed.

"They usually come right up close. And usually there are loads of them. Usually …" Fin's voice trailed off. "I don't know where they are."

They waited. Fin played his tune on his penny whistle and still they waited. Like kings of the castle they watched the surface of the sea. The fiery sun came fully up. The slow-winged heron left his place on the rock and flew silently overhead. But no seals came to sing for them.

"Sorry, Tarkin," Fin said after several silent minutes, "they usually come. Honestly."

"No worries, man. Maybe they're off singing for someone else."

"Aye, I suppose they could be."

"Or fishing for their breakfast?"

Fin shrugged his shoulders. It seemed strange. The seals always sang to him in the morning.

"Or maybe they don't like old weirdo winkle picker over there?" Tarkin nodded in the direction of the man with the bright yellow coat, who had shifted to work on the rocks near the cave. "Or maybe," he continued, his voice dropping, "they don't like me?"

"No, Tarkin. Course they like you." But the thought did flit through Magnus Fin's mind as he looked at his loud friend.

"They've probably slept in," Fin said, trying to make a joke but not managing a laugh with it. Then his eyes fell to the edge of the rock, the spot he'd been avoiding for ten minutes. The letter M was still there; if anything it was brighter than it had been the day before. He peered down to the ledge that jutted under it. F was still there too. He gulped, looked to the next rock and gulped again. He could see more M Fs scratched into the smooth grey stone. He shivered and bit his nail. The scary feeling he'd been pushing away came rushing back. Way in the distance the winkle picker walked along the beach path, his pail swinging by his side.

"Jeepers creepers," said Tarkin, only now seeing the white letters inscribed on the rocks. "Something wants you, Magnus Fin – that's for sure. Your initials are all over the place."

Fin frowned. "Um, yeah – it gives me the creeps. They're everywhere." It was true. The rock writer had been back, and busy.

"Well, he's got to be around here somewhere." Tarkin's voice rang with a sense of adventure. Both boys looked far along the shore to where the winkle picker was bending down. Then they looked at each other.

"It's him, Fin, it's got to be. Come on! Let's ask him what he's up to?"

"No, Tarkin. Don't ask him. Come back!" Approaching the stranger was the last thing Magnus Fin wanted to do, but already Tarkin was jumping off the rock and slithering over the seaweed.

"Wait for me," Fin shouted, not wanting to be left alone either. He jumped off the high rock and ran after Tarkin. In the distance the winkle picker hunched down on the flat rocks. He must have heard the boys this time for he looked up then hurried to his feet. Picking up his pail, he shuffled quickly away.

Tarkin, being taller, could jump further. Fin lagged behind and let Tarkin go on ahead. Balanced on a large grey boulder Fin stopped and looked around. The winkle picker had disappeared. "Come back," Fin shouted. "Tarkin! Come back!" but his voice was against the wind. Tarkin didn't hear him.

By this time Tarkin had reached the shelf of flat rocks. Fin watched as Tarkin dropped to his knees, just as the winkle picker had done. A horrible sense of foreboding took hold of Magnus Fin. Something was up; he just knew it. He felt it in his selkie heart.

Now Tarkin had risen to his feet. Fin watched him cup his hands to his mouth and shout, "Go back, Fin!

Don't look!" Tarkin was holding up his hands now to ward off his friend. But Magnus Fin, like someone walking in their sleep, moved forward, coming closer and closer to the flat rocks where Tarkin was standing, shouting at the top of his voice, "No, Fin! Don't come any closer!"

Chapter 5

Magnus Fin knew what he would see before he reached the flat rocks. He kept walking even though Tarkin was almost hoarse with shouting for him to go back. The smell reached him and sickened him. Tarkin was trying to block the awful sight. But it was no good. Magnus Fin drew level with his friend and stared down to where three dead seals lay side by side on the flat rock. They weren't pups but large grey seals. Magnus Fin closed his eyes and stumbled as though he might faint. Tarkin grabbed his arm and tried to pull Fin away.

"Hey, Fin, let's get out of here. Race you up the brae to school, buddy ..." But Tarkin's words fluttered around him like the wind.

Magnus Fin stared down at the bodies of the seals, the stench of death and seaweed clinging to the back of his throat. He could see no marks on their bodies. He fell to his knees and touched their fur. It was warm. They hadn't been dead long. What had happened to them?

"Maybe it was that winkle picker," Tarkin said, edging back and looking anxiously up the coast in the direction he had gone. "Hey, Fin," he said nervously, "let's get out of here. There's something weird going on and I don't like it. Not one bit."

"But what happened to them?" That's all Fin could say. He said it over and over, shaking his head, not able to pull his eyes away.

"Fin, I don't know and I don't much feel like finding out. Old age, maybe? Like my granddad; you know, it happens."

"But not like this," Magnus Fin said, still stroking the fur of the three creatures, first one then another. "They're not old. They're young. These seals are about five years old, and they're strong – or they were. They should be swimming under the sea. Not lying here dead."

Now that Tarkin looked properly he could tell these seals weren't old. Their skins were sleek and their faces were smooth, but a film lay over their blank eyes. "You know what Sargent's like if we're late. Come on, Fin, let's split."

Magnus Fin looked slowly up at his friend. "Something's wrong under the sea, Tarkin. They're calling me; I know it. See their white eyes? I've got to go." Fin got to his feet.

"Poor things," said Tarkin, and for a moment the two boys just stared down in silence. "Are they selkies, do you think?"

Fin shrugged his shoulders. "I don't know."

They left the three dead seals lying side by side on the flat rock. A crow squawked and circled overhead.

Magnus Fin and Tarkin walked in silence along the beach. Even if they'd felt like eating, there was no time for breakfast. Any minute now the school bell would ring. They hurried along the harbour road then up the hill towards school.

"Take me under the sea with you, Fin," Tarkin blurted out at last, breaking the silence.

"Tarkin – you can't even swim."

Tarkin shrugged his shoulders and twisted his earring around. For once he was stumped for an answer. Magnus Fin had been trying hard to teach his friend to swim for four months. Tarkin's legs were too long or his arms too uncoordinated perhaps, but he could only manage three strokes at the most then he would start thrashing about and sink.

"And," Fin added, "you can't breathe underwater."

"OK, I get it. You're the special one." There was hurt in his voice. "So, when are you planning on going?"

"Soon. I don't know." Fin shrugged his shoulders. He looked confused. "At the next low tide I suppose."

"When's that?"

Fin knew his tide tables. He read them like other people read comics. "Half past six tonight. And, Tarkin," he added, "I didn't ask to be special." He thumped Tarkin gently on the arm. "I would take you with me if I could."

Tarkin nodded as though he understood. "I know. But, like, won't it be freezing?"

"My wetsuit's thick," Fin said, "and maybe I've got selkie blood and blubber!" With not an ounce of fat on him it was supposed to be a joke, but with the memory of the three dead seals heavy between them they didn't laugh.

It wasn't the cold, though, that was worrying Magnus Fin. It was the thought of what he might meet under the sea. Last time, he'd been forced to fight a terrible sea monster. He thankfully came back safe and sound, but poor Aquella lost her seal skin. He took a deep breath and glanced at Tarkin. His friend looked glum. Fin knew the swimming thing was hard for Tarkin.

He dived into his pocket and fished out the sand glass he'd found first thing that morning. "Wee present for you, Tark," he said, handing it to him.

"Hey – sand glass. Cool!" Tarkin looked through it, just as Magnus Fin had done. Maybe it was the unexpected gift, or something he saw magnified through it, but suddenly Tarkin brightened up. He pocketed the glass carefully then swung his rucksack through the air.

"Come on, M F," he said. "If you're gonna save the seals, T here's gonna help you. That's what friends are for. Come on, buddy, race you to school!"

Chapter 6

Magnus Fin was quiet in school all that day. They were doing the ancient Egyptians which he really liked, but today he couldn't concentrate. Tarkin saved him three times. They had a code for passing answers, which Sargent hadn't cracked yet. It wasn't that Magnus Fin was slow. It was just that his mind was often on other subjects, like things under the sea. He sat up and listened, though, when Mr Sargent spoke about tombs and pharaohs and lost cities beneath the waves.

"There are many sunken cities in the world," the teacher said, sweeping his arm across the map, most of which was coloured blue, meaning ocean. "Lost continents even." Fin's eyes grew wide as pancakes. For the first time that day he forgot about the three dead seals and the underwater journey that lay ahead. Sunken cities! Wow! Sunken continents!

"Like Atlantis?" Retha asked.

"Well done, Retha, clever girl. Exactly. Like Atlantis."

Tarkin glanced across at Magnus Fin. It was rare for Fin to put his hand up in class, but he did. "Are there any up here?" he asked, his mind now brimming with sunken palaces, churches, underwater streets and watery houses.

"Good question, bo— I mean Magnus – um Fin. Divers, it seems, don't like cold northern turbulent waters. Lots of sunken cities have been discovered in the sea off the coasts of India and Egypt, but very little research has been done up here. Too blooming cold. Ha-ha!"

Magnus Fin went back to his dreaming after that, but the thought of finding an underwater city comforted him. Just think of all the treasures he'd find down there! They'd have to flit to a bigger house. He'd need a huge room for all that treasure …

"Fin!"

Then maybe he'd find a sunken harbour of ships as well.

"Psst! Magnus Fin!"

School was over. The bell had rung. The classroom was empty apart from Magnus Fin sitting there staring into space. Tarkin had his jacket on and his new stripy scarf tied round his neck. He was prodding Magnus Fin and eating a banana. "Come on, Fin. You don't want the janitor to lock you in."

Fin shook himself awake and scrambled to his feet. "Race you down the brae," he said, and dashed out of the classroom, leaving Tarkin staring after him with a half-eaten banana in his hand.

Fin was fast today, faster even than long-legged Tarkin. As he raced pell-mell down the brae, images of sunken cities, dead seals, sunken ships and swaying forests of seaweed played like a film in his head. Tarkin was gaining on him. Fin ran faster, his arms pumping furiously back and forth. What kind of help, he wondered, was Tarkin planning? Should he tell Aquella? Should he tell his dad? And would Miranda be there to meet him when he opened the door to the sea?

"Gotcha!" Tarkin caught up with him. He was panting hard and fumbling in his pocket. "You dropped something," he said, thrusting a small white and orange stone into Fin's hand, "and I bet it'll come in handy for this mission you've got ahead of you."

Fin stared down at his open palm. In it lay his moon-stone: the stone his father had given him when he first went under the sea to help the selkies. It was his bravery stone that he always wore around his neck. He couldn't believe that today of all days the lace it dangled from had broken. He curled his fingers around the moon-stone and smiled broadly at his friend.

"You've helped me already, Tark." Fin's green eye shone as he felt strength and excitement pour into him. "Thanks a million."

"No worries, man," Tarkin said, panting and flicking strands of hair out of his eyes. "I'm happy to help."

"Well, you could come and wait for me if you want, tonight when I go under the sea? You could sit on the rocks. And bring some of that toffee your mum's always buying you. It would feel better under the sea if I had your mum's toffee to think about."

Tarkin grinned. "Sure, buddy, I'll be there. I'll stuff my pockets full of toffees. And I'll bring the torch, and a blanket. Hey, I'm in on the moonlight mission. How cool is that?"

"But, Tarkin," Fin said, pocketing the precious moon-stone and biting his lip, "don't try and swim after me. Please don't do that. Do you promise?"

Tarkin put his hand to his heart and solemnly promised. "Course not, buddy," he said, winking. Then the two boys walked along the harbour road to the bridge. Tarkin started chanting one of the Native American protection spells he had learned back home, and Magnus Fin hoped it really would protect him.

"See ya soon," Tarkin said when they parted at the bridge.

Fin glanced at his watch then waved. The tide would be fully out in two and a half hours time. Walking back along the track to the cottage he felt dizzy with excitement. It had been dangerous the first time he had gone under the sea. He gulped remembering just how scary it had been. Fin felt the excitement tighten into fear. "You have to go," he said to himself, "and it'll be fine." But he still felt anxious.

So he thought of the three dead seals. He thought of the letters M F written on the rocks. He thought of his beautiful grandmother Miranda. He was being called, and he, Magnus Fin, would go.

Chapter 7

At five o'clock Magnus Fin pulled on his wetsuit. Unusually the cottage down by the sea was empty. His mother worked in the jewellers in town. Perhaps, thought Magnus, she'd missed the bus. His father was still up at the farm bringing the cows in for the winter and the last of the hay inside. Aquella, whose music teacher had discovered she had a good singing voice *and* could play the clarsach, was at her band practice. In any case, Fin had decided it would be easier not to tell Aquella exactly when he was going. It was hard enough for her being a selkie with no seal skin, learning to be a land girl, sleeping in a bed and walking on pavements. She didn't need more to worry about.

So Fin was alone, and feeling more nervous by the minute. Dressed in his wetsuit he sat at the kitchen table and ate one of those pasta dinners you heat up and eat all by yourself. He wasn't hungry, but it might be a long time before he would eat again, and the pasta would give him warmth and energy.

He had tied his moon-stone to a new leather lace and it now hung around his neck. He glanced out of the window. In twenty minutes it would be low tide, and already it was dark. As he played with his food he spoke to himself, trying to pump himself up with courage. "You'll be fine, Magnus Fin. You're half selkie, half human. You're half child, half man. *Sliochan Nan Ronnie* or something like that – that's you – special! Something's up under the sea and you're being called."

Suddenly from outside he heard three short whoops. That could only be Tarkin. Fin looked around the room, wishing he could find a sudden surge of excitement. The fire was out. The clock ticked loudly. Seconds dragged. Time, Fin knew, moved differently under the sea. A minute on land could feel like a day under the sea. How long, he wondered, would he be gone this time? Slowly Fin got up and with a sense of dread left the cottage and went out into the night.

All the excitement was in Tarkin. "Wow! Cool wetsuit man. You look like a real diver."

Fin scowled. "I am."

"Well, let's go, diver! We've got eleven minutes." Tarkin was hopping from foot to foot.

"We?"

"OK, OK, you."

Tarkin had brought a torch, a blanket, a flask of hot chocolate, a thick towel, plus his pockets were stuffed with toffees. His enthusiasm was contagious and soon Magnus Fin's gloomy mood lifted and he was jogging along beside Tarkin.

"You think of everything, Tark," Fin said, running in the path of light from Tarkin's torch.

"Yeah, I know. Oh, man, I am just so excited."

Magnus Fin was beginning to feel the same, but even so, as they clambered over the rocks Fin wished that he was the one holding the torch and Tarkin the one wearing the wetsuit. Why couldn't it be him sitting on the rock chanting protection spells and stuffing himself with toffee while Tarkin went under the sea?

"Boy oh boy, we're here," Tarkin shouted, "with half a minute to go. I'll do the countdown. Get ready, M F."

Magnus Fin kicked off his trainers, curled his toes over the edge of the black rock and stared down into the dark, swirling water.

Tarkin wrapped himself in a fleecy blanket and got comfortable on top of the rock. He put his flask and a small pile of toffees by his side then started to shout, "Ten! Nine! Eight!"

Magnus Fin took a deep breath. The moon glinted like coins on the black water.

"Seven! Six! Five!" Tarkin shone his torch down onto the water.

Fin thought of the three dead seals. He thought of the writing on the rocks. He thought of his grandmother.

"Four! Three! Two!" Tarkin's voice was rising with excitement.

Fin thought about himself – half a selkie – called under the water. He bent his knees and swung his arms back. This was it. It was now or never.

"One! Jump!"

Fin didn't move. His knees quaked. He bit his lip. It looked so dark down there, and cold.

"JUMP!" Tarkin yelled. "Jump or I'll push you!"

Magnus Fin jumped, splashing into the freezing sea. His hand groped through the water to find the shell handle of the door that led to the selkie's underwater world. Grasping it, he pulled and immediately felt himself being sucked through, into a flash of bright emerald-green light. The light was blinding, the sound that filled his ears rushing. His lungs felt fit to burst.

Then a change came over him, and Magnus Fin could breathe under the sea. And though the beam of light from Tarkin's torch penetrated downwards through the water, it was nothing to the light that shone out from the blue pupils of Magnus Fin's eyes. He blinked, and brilliant silvery beams of light stretched through the sea.

He kicked and dived deeper. A thrill shot through his whole body. *I'm home again*, he thought, *I'm home under the sea!* And the fear that had weighed on him all day was gone.

Through the swirling water Fin spied a tiny crab. It was clinging to the other side of the rock door and appeared to be waiting for him. For a second the crab looked up at Fin then scuttled off, across the rock and through the water, its small legs paddling frantically like oars. A shudder of recognition ran through Fin as he pushed himself away from the black rock. Was this the crab he had last seen heading into the debris of the monster's awful crumbling palace?

The crab stopped paddling and turned around. *That's right,* he said, answering Fin's thoughts. *We meet again.*

Perhaps it was the memory of how brave this crab had been during his last mission, but Fin instantly trusted it.

For such a tiny thing it moved fast. Fin kicked his feet and stretched his arms wide, gliding forward. The crab darted in and out between fronds of seaweed. Sometimes the crab shot a glance behind to make sure Magnus Fin was following. He was. He didn't know what else to do. Fin had forgotten how easily he moved through the water. What a sense of freedom he felt to be deep under the sea again. Forests of algae and seaweed waved to him like long lost friends. The fish that swam past seemed to flick their tails in welcome. His selkie heart thrilled. As Magnus Fin swam on and gazed around him, he wondered why he had felt afraid of this wonderful watery world.

This is the best place ever, Fin thought, gliding onwards, kicking his feet and smiling from ear to ear.

Chapter 8

Still following the sometimes scuttling, sometimes paddling crab, Magnus Fin dived deeper. Now he found himself swimming through a long valley. Just like on the land, so under the sea there were rocks, mountains, forests and valleys. On the sandy floor of this valley a forest of kelp swayed to and fro with the tide. Fin swam above it, brushing the seaweed tips with his feet. He felt how the current rocked him from side to side. It was no good trying to resist it. Quickly he learnt to move with the rhythm of the water, like the fish that were now staring at him, or darting past, or tickling his feet.

The crab that Fin had been following for a long time or a short time, he couldn't tell which, stopped and crawled under a clam shell. Wherever Fin was being led, he had now arrived. With his heart thudding loudly he swept his bright eye-lights through the dark water. Tall craggy rocks, covered with barnacles, surrounded him. Great ancient faces, or so it seemed, stared at him. He was in an underwater world of cliffs, craters and canyons. Ahead of him loomed a huge circular rock. The crab had brought Fin to this place for a reason – but what was it? He didn't know whether to swim on or tread water and wait for something to happen.

Booming, sighing and slapping sounds surrounded

him, echoing on and on. From somewhere a muffled banging noise like a bass drum thundered. Fin twisted his body round, looking behind and above as he did so, but where the sounds came from he couldn't tell. He circled his arms and kicked his feet. Why did the crab have to leave him like that? The banging went on. It sent shivers through Fin's whole body. Something was bound to happen soon.

I've come, he called out in his selkie thoughts. *M F, that's me. I'm here. I came.*

Still nothing. *At least the crab is close by*, Fin thought. That gave him some comfort, but when he scanned the valley floor the clam shell had vanished. He groaned and grasped his moon-stone. That helped to still his thudding heart. He circled his feet, glancing first at one rock face, than another, not noticing the brown liquid that stained the water and snaked around him.

Through the water Fin imagined he could see a face, like a great Native American chief, beckoning him from the huge round rock. Not knowing where else to go, Fin swam towards the stern face. Only then did he smell the stench. He twisted round. Some foul-smelling creature was nearby. He looked up, down. But nothing was there, nothing but rocks and water. Even the face had vanished. Fin stared at the rock. Thick brown droplets oozed into the sea.

Magnus Fin felt his eyes smart. He rubbed them and felt thick slime smear the back of his hands. He could see now that this brown sludge, whatever it was, dripped from a tiny crack in the rock. As it dripped it polluted the sea. And – Fin covered his mouth and nose – it stank! He swam forwards, wanting and not wanting to explore, afraid of what he might find. Fin curled his fingers around his moon-stone. *Don't turn back now*, he thought, spurring himself on.

Up close, he could see that this rock was weeping thick brown tears. What he had imagined as the eye of an American chief was a hole in the rock from which the tears were seeping.

Fin's eyes were still smarting and for a second his torch-lights dimmed. He blinked and shook his head, struggling to keep his eyes open. Not only his eyes hurt but so did his ears. A dull repetitive banging hammered in his head, as though something or someone was pounding the sea with a battering ram.

Was the thudding noise coming from inside his head or behind this weeping rock? Fighting a splitting headache, Magnus Fin dug his fingers into the crevices and hoisted himself level with the hole in the rock. The banging noise ceased. He pressed his face up to the crack and forced himself to peer through.

A green eye peered back at him! It was the most menacing eye he had ever seen. A bolt of panic shot through him. He wanted to cry out. Fin kicked backwards away from the ghastly staring thing.

His courage drained away. In a panic he thrashed his arms and legs wildly through the water, wanting only to swim as far away as possible. His eyes stung. Half blindly he lashed out. Why had the mysterious little crab led him to such a place? And where was the crab now?

Fin thought of Tarkin, sitting waiting on the black rock. He wanted to be back on the land. This world was too frightening, full of strange creatures. And the smell was terrible!

45

Quick! Hold on to me. It was Miranda.

Fin reached up and grabbed hold of her tail fins. Above him the water spun like a whirlpool and Fin was tossed up in the churning currents. In seconds the weeping rock was far behind. Fin, clutching on for dear life, was whisked away at great speed in and out of coves, caverns and past giant cliffs. A deep whooshing sound almost deafened him. The swaying kelp forests below blurred with the sheer speed of Miranda's swimming.

Only when they reached the far end of the oceanic canyon, where the rock formations opened out into vast sandy plains, did Miranda slow down. She twisted her head now to look into her grandson's eyes. He was flushed and shaking.

Why did you come here, Fin? she asked, not unkindly but with concern in her voice.

Magnus Fin released his hold on Miranda's tail fins and floated in the water beside her. *But, I – I thought you called me? I saw the writing on the rocks, and …*

I didn't call you, Fin. Not now. Now is not a good time for you to be here.

Magnus Fin looked quizzically at his grandmother, this great silvery seal with glittering green eyes. She was the strong mother of the selkies, known as the bright one.

But why? Miranda, what's wrong?

She shook her head sadly. *It's nothing, Fin. The sickness has come to us, that's all. It'll pass like all things pass. The crab should mind his own business. Now tell me, how is Aquella? And how is my son Ragnor? How is life up there on the land, Magnus Fin?* As she questioned him Miranda

46

nudged Fin forward and pushed him swiftly upwards through the water.

Aquella's fine. She says to tell you she likes school. She's in a girl's band you know. Dad works on a farm. You'd never know he was a selkie now.

Good, Fin, that's good. And you? You have a best friend now?

On and upwards they travelled, Miranda gently nuzzling her grandson, until the rays of moonlight stretched down through the sea and the water felt lighter.

Yes, that's Tarkin. He's on the rock waiting for me. He's from America. He brought toffee and a torch.

And there it was, not a ray of moonlight but the beam of Tarkin's torch, penetrating the water from the world above. His grandmother had led him back to the door in the black rock and opened it with a push of her flipper. *Go then, dear one, go back, don't worry about us, and Neptune bless you.*

In a flash, Miranda flicked her tail and dived deep under the water. At the same moment Fin broke through the surface of the sea with a gasp.

Tarkin had dropped down on his belly with his arms dropping over the side of the rock. "Oh, boy, am I glad you're here. Grab my hands, Fin. I left you some toffee. Come on. Welcome back, buddy."

Soon Magnus Fin was huddled in the warm fleece blanket. With Tarkin's towel wrapped around his damp head he stuffed two toffees into his mouth. The strange encounter under the sea faded for a moment as though it had never happened.

"So, Fin, what happened? You were gone all of two minutes. Like, I want to hear all about it."

Fin stared at Tarkin then stared down at the sea. It was lapping around the rock. "Nothing much happened," he said, chewing busily. "Nothing at all."

"Nothing much? Come on, Fin, something must have happened!"

Fin looked over his shoulder and stared again out to sea. It was dark and cold. Fragments of memory, like a dream half-recalled, came to him. Goose bumps crawled across his flesh. He swallowed the toffees then murmured, "A green staring eye, creepy, and banging. I got scared. And Miranda came. Fast. You, I told her your name. Sickness Miranda said. It's come, nothing to worry about." Fin turned back to look at Tarkin and shrugged. "I think that's what happened."

"She's trying to protect you, Fin." Tarkin jumped up. "That horrible banging noise? Well, I heard it too. No joke! I was sitting here all alone. I was just tearing off a toffee wrapper when I heard it. I got the creepiest muckle feeling all over me. It was coming from under the water – I heard it, honest!"

Fin could tell it was true by the way Tarkin's eyes blazed and his voice trembled. The torch was shining on him, lighting up his pale shocked face and his wide blue eyes.

"You look like you heard a ghost," Fin said. He pulled on his trainers and managed a weak smile. "Look, we'd better get home. Don't worry, it's just some illness. Miranda said it'll pass and everything will be fine." Fin stood up and shone the torch down onto the foot ledges.

"So what about that creepy eye then?" Tarkin scooped up the flask and blanket.

"Maybe I was imagining it. Come on, forget it. I want to go home."

"Well, what about all this writing? Something's up and you know it." Tarkin shone his torch down onto the hundreds of Ms and Fs. "You're needed, and your grandmother's trying to protect you. You can't deny that, Fin. If it was me I'd go back."

Magnus Fin jumped off the rock. "But you're not me, Tarkin," he shouted. "You're not half selkie. You didn't come eye to eye with that scary wild thing down there. You don't know what it's like." With hot tears stinging his eyes, Fin leapt over the rocks in the moonlight and ran home.

Chapter 9

Early next morning, Magnus Fin sloshed cold water on his face and stared at himself in the mirror. One green eye and one brown eye stared back and a blank face that didn't seem to have any answers. "It'll come to you in your dreams," that's what Tarkin had said the night before when he'd finally caught up with Fin on the beach path.

Fin sighed. Nothing was coming to him. Sometimes the thing he longed for was to be normal. He'd confided that to Tarkin, who of course, all fired up for adventure, had talked him out of that. "Normal? Man oh man! Do you know what you're saying? Life is way too exciting to veg out and bleat. Normal? I can't imagine anything worse. Get real, Fin. Get unique! And anyway – you're needed."

"Am I?" Fin asked his reflection, running his fingers through his hair.

"Breakfast's ready, children," his mother Barbara shouted up the stairs. Magnus Fin dried his face. He could smell the toast. He could hear his cousin Aquella clattering about in her little attic room. He didn't know getting dressed still felt strange to her. He didn't know at that same moment she was staring at her reflection in her mirror, and running a plump finger over the cotton of her school uniform, then over her white soft skin, thinking how this face, these clothes, this arm, weren't her real self. Magnus Fin guessed at none of that. He glanced at his face in the mirror, managed a half-smile then went down to the kitchen.

For the first time in ages Magnus Fin didn't run off to the beach. He sat down at the table for breakfast.

"Not off beachcombing?" Barbara asked, sliding the jar of raspberry jam towards him and giving him a quizzical look. "I mean, it's really nice to have your company, but I thought you always went beachcombing before school?"

"No, I think I've got enough stuff."

Barbara and Aquella stopped chewing and stared at him.

"But, Fin," Aquella said gently, "today might be the day you get a bell from the *Titanic*."

"Or a coin from the Spanish Armada," his mother added, studying him for signs of illness.

Fin let his toast fall onto his plate. He looked up at them both then blurted out, "Well, you go then! Why don't you? Both of you! You go!" His eyes welled up with tears. He pushed the chair back, grabbed his rucksack and ran out of the house.

He sped down the track, his heart pounding. He heard his mother shouting, "Fin, Magnus Fin, what's wrong? I didn't mean to upset you. I'm sorry, Fin. Come back!" But he didn't turn round. He kept going till he couldn't hear her any more. Then when he reached the bridge he didn't turn left towards school but ran up through the field.

He couldn't stand it any more. Life had been so good. He had a best friend. And he had Aquella. And his parents were happy. And now something was up under the sea. Seals were dying, he didn't know what to do about it, and anyway it seemed he wasn't wanted. So what about the M Fs? And that horrid green eye? He thought all this as he ran up through the barley fields towards the farm where his dad worked. His dad would know what to do. Fin would tell him everything. On he ran. He could smell the dung now and see the long-horned Highland cows. Still a thousand thoughts raced through his head. He didn't want to worry Aquella. He knew that if the seals were in trouble she'd want to go down there and help – but without a seal skin she couldn't. Only he, Magnus Fin, it seemed, could do that.

By this time he had reached the farm. In the distance he could see the noisy tractor with its long forked pick-up with a bale of hay on the end, and driving the tractor was his dad.

Fin waved and jumped up and down. "Dad! Hey, Dad! It's me. It's Fin! I've come to give you a hand with your work!"

But the tractor was huge and the radio was blaring and Fin, by comparison, was very small. The big red tractor drove right past him into a shed where mounds of hay bales were stacked up. Fin ran after it then watched as the huge fork dumped the hay bale. Ragnor didn't get out but reversed the tractor and headed back to the field. Fin couldn't believe it. Was he that small? His own father hadn't seen him!

He slumped down on a pallet and leant back against the hay to get his breath back. From the shed he watched the tractor heave up another bale of hay. It all had to be stored before the winter. A thought suddenly occurred to Magnus Fin. *Thought transmission!* His father, though he'd been on the land for many years now, was, deep down, a selkie, wasn't he? Fin had never tried it before but it just might work. Fin closed his eyes and thought hard. He concentrated on his dad and imagined his thoughts swimming towards him. Here goes, he thought, and said inside:

Something's not good under the sea. But Miranda says not to worry. What do you think, Dad?

Jings! Fin! I thought that was the radio. I almost fell out of the tractor.

Sorry.

That's OK. I'm a bit rusty at this kind of thing. Well, son, with me for a dad life was never going to be straightforward.

Dad, she says the sickness has come to them. I can't think about anything else.

The sickness! There was silence, as though a phone had been dropped.

Dad?

I'm here. Son, if Miranda says to stay away that's what you should do. She knows best.

But Ragnor didn't sound so sure. Magnus Fin was silent for a while.

But Dad, I feel I should go. Tarkin thinks she's just saying that to protect me.

It might pass to you, son. These sicknesses can be fatal.

Just then Ragnor drove his tractor into the shed with a huge bale of hay jabbed onto the prongs of the pick-up.

Hey, Dad, I'm right in front of you!

Ragnor tooted the horn and waved to his son. Then

he leant out of the tractor and shouted, "Want to drive a tractor?"

Magnus Fin nodded, clambered up and sat next to his father. In no time Fin was busy pushing levers, changing gear, and later on, holding the steering wheel.

"You should be at school, you know, son," Ragnor said, though Fin could tell by the way he said it that he wasn't about to march him back to school. Not today. It was as though Ragnor was glad for his son's company, glad perhaps for the chance to tell him more about his selkie ancestors. "But now you're here, well, you might as well stay."

Magnus Fin grinned and was just about to break open a bag of crisps when a shadow passed over his father's face and he spoke, his voice so low it was hard to hear him over the rumble of the engine. "The sickness," Ragnor said, "has been before." Ragnor manoeuvred the tractor along a rutted track as he spoke. "And no doubt it will come again. Why don't you just forget it, Fin? Enjoy your life. You've already saved our selkie family once, and you've got yourself a good pal. Next year you'll be going up to the high school. You've got a whole life ahead of you. Don't spoil it now."

Magnus Fin stared at his father, with his jet-black hair and shining dark eyes, the strong man from the sea who came ashore and married Fin's mother. Ragnor the selkie was telling Magnus Fin to forget it!

"But I *want* to go back to the sea," Fin blurted out, realising in that moment that he really did, scary green eye or not. "They need me to help them, Dad, and I want to go. I'm *Sliochan Nan Ronnie*. Aquella said I was."

Ragnor shook his head and laughed. "*Ron*, son. *Sliochan Nan Ron*." He stared at his son, his handsome rugged face a blend of sadness and admiration. "Aye, she's right. You are. But, Fin – first hear my story. It's not for nothing Miranda is afraid."

Chapter 10

Ragnor switched the engine off. It was lunchtime and the other farm labourers had stopped work. Ragnor turned to look at his son, then spoke in a low voice, "Your grandmother, my mother, is the most beautiful and brave seal in the ocean. You know they call her the bright one? And there are too many who want to hunt the bright one."

"Why would anybody want to do that?"

"Good question, son." Ragnor shrugged. "Mostly she stays in the deep waters, a queen among selkies."

"Does that make you a prince?"

Ragnor shook his head and laughed. "No, Fin. In the selkie kingdom you are not born a queen or a prince. It is something you achieve. Selkies who do brave deeds to help others, they can become kings and queens, princes and princesses. You perhaps are a prince, but not me. Aquella may well be a princess; but me? I'm happy to be a farm labourer and to be the husband of Barbara, your father and Aquella's uncle. I'm a simple land selkie – that's all."

Ragnor gazed ahead as though it was the deep green sea in front of him and not a stubble field. "Miranda was a queen long before I was born," he went on. "If selkies learn the secret of shape-shifting they live till a grand age. And no one knows it better than she." He looked at his son, his handsome face serious. "The great change is no easy thing, Fin. Oh, great Neptune no! Many selkies lose their lives shape-shifting. But Miranda?" At this Ragnor fell silent till Magnus Fin was afraid he wouldn't carry on with his story.

Fin prodded his dad on the arm. "Miranda?" he asked, waiting. "What about Miranda?"

Ragnor shook his head, as though waking from a dream. "Aye, Miranda," he said at last, "well, her story is also my story. You see, Fin, she taught me to change out of my seal skin into human form at will. She had the wisdom to change whenever she wanted. She didn't have to wait for the change times – midwinter and midsummer. She taught me many things: to swim with the tides; to play the surf waves; to rescue fishermen in difficulties; and to steer clear of great white sharks and killer whales. And she taught me the songs to release my seal skin and hide it in safe places. Then, when I fell in love with Barbara, a human woman, and the other selkies said I was foolish, Miranda said only one thing – follow your heart.

"Then every other day and every other night after first meeting your mother I changed out of my seal skin and came ashore. And when my uncles and cousins refused to swim with me and hunt with me, thinking, by loving a human I had betrayed them, still Miranda didn't heed them. She stayed by me. Follow your heart, Ragnor, that's what she told me.

"You see," he said, his voice dropping to a whisper, "she had followed hers." Ragnor grew silent, so silent it seemed his story was done.

"And then what happened?" Fin asked after the silence became unbearable. "What happened to Miranda?"

Ragnor blinked. "Everyone said to take a mate from the great Atlantic selkies was madness. It was well known they were reckless. They fished in the very waters the whalers and trawlermen fished. They bit through their nets. They taunted killer whales then outwitted them. But Miranda followed her heart. Her mate was the strongest of the great Atlantic selkies. Together they travelled to the Arctic and back and many adventures they had, your grandmother and grandfather. Often Miranda told me about my father. How brave he was. How he was known in all the northern waters as the fearless one. How he could leap a twenty-foot wave and sing with a rich, deep voice that, once heard, you'd never forget. Except ..." Ragnor paused, "... I never heard him. Miranda found him dead the day I was born. It was the sickness."

Fin thought about his grandfather, a great Atlantic selkie. He imagined this magnificent creature leaping high waves and swimming beside Miranda.

Ragnor turned to look at his son. "His name was Fin."

For a while, nothing more was said. Fin gazed out at the field.

"So now you've heard the story, son. You know why Miranda wants to protect you. It's a terrible thing, this sickness. The selkies have long been persecuted, but when the sickness comes there is no one to fight, no one to hide from. We don't even know what causes it."

Fin nodded. If anything, his father's story had made him even more determined to go back under the sea to try and help his selkie family. He was sure now that he had been summoned for a reason; the brown sludge and the green eye flashed before his eyes. He didn't want any more members of his family to die from this terrible sickness.

Ragnor knew that look in his son's eyes. He placed a hand on his shoulder. "The truth is, son, life would be easier for you if you forgot the sea. Much easier. But, if you still want to go, then go." He closed his eyes and sighed. "Take your moon-stone with you and heed your instinct." He put his hand to his belly as though that's where instinct came from.

Solemnly Fin nodded.

After that, nothing more was said on the subject. They ate cheddar cheese and chutney sandwiches and after lunch they brought in the last of the hay, piling it high in the byre. Sometimes they laughed. Sometimes they were silent. Fin felt the strength of his father and of the land seep into him.

Before Magnus Fin went upstairs to get ready for bed that night his mother had been extra loving and given him a long hug. He felt warm and happy inside. Now he was back at the mirror brushing his teeth, looking for bravery in his face and finding it this time.

His toothbrush caught on something. The white toothpaste turned red and Magnus Fin spat out his last baby tooth. He held it between his thumb and forefinger, washed his mouth out, then winked at himself with his brown eye. If ever he needed a good omen for this mission that lay ahead of him, here it was.

Granny May up in John O'Groats was always going on about the tooth fairy. She said the last tooth to fall was the most special. Pure magic, that's what she called it. Only the other week she'd seen Fin wobble his last tooth. She'd laughed and told him he could wish on a last tooth and that wish would surely come true.

Well, Miranda, Fin's other granny, was as magical as any tooth fairy. Miranda often gave him gifts, tossing him treasures on the incoming tide. He would give her something this time: a baby tooth from her grandson. And not just any baby tooth, but his last one! That might help the sickness. Didn't Granny May say this tooth could cure all ills? Fin held the tooth between his thumb and forefinger and brought it close up to the mirror. Perhaps it was the light from the candle flickering by the glass, but that small sharp tooth gleamed like a nugget of gold.

Magnus Fin lay his head down on his pillow that night and smiled. Underneath it lay his lucky tooth and his moon-stone. In his heart he had the story of his grandfather. And in his belly he had his instinct. He had checked the tide tables and laid out his wetsuit. He was ready.

That awful green eye had something to do with the sickness of the seals, Fin was sure of it. The crab had guided him towards it for a reason. Well, the very next evening, he would go back. And he wouldn't allow himself to be nuzzled back up to the surface this time.

Chapter 11

While Magnus Fin was preparing to go under the sea, Tarkin, if he managed to work on his mother's boyfriend and if everything went according to plan, would be *on* the sea.

Frank, the boyfriend, had, back at the end of summer, acquired a small wooden boat. There was just one problem. Tarkin didn't like Frank. In fact, Tarkin couldn't stand Frank. Frank wasn't Tarkin's dad. Tarkin's real dad had a real fishing boat. Tarkin's real dad had taken him fishing when they lived in the Yukon. Tarkin had gone on about it so much that one day Frank turned up with a broad smile on his face and a twinkle in his eyes. "Come to the window and see what I bought us, buddy," he said, waving Tarkin over.

"I'm not your buddy." That's what Tarkin had said, until his mother started to cry, saying did he have any idea how hurtful he was being? Tarkin hated it when she cried. He wasn't being hurtful. He was just telling the truth. But he was kind of interested in what was outside the window. So Tarkin stood up, pretending he was looking for the remote control. While Frank was comforting his mother Tarkin shot a glance out the window. Wow! A boat! But he said nothing, switched on the television and ignored Frank.

"That cost Frank a lot of money, Tarkin. It don't grow on trees, you know. Frank got the boat for you and him. He thought you'd like it," said his mother.

"I like it," Tarkin said, then muttered, "big shame about him."

"What did you say, son?"

But Frank took her hand and squeezed it. "Hey, it's OK, Martha. He says he likes it. That's good. That's just fine."

That had been three months ago. Since then the boat had bobbed about down in the harbour with nothing but rain and an occasional seagull in it. Frank had made a few hints about taking the boat out together, but Tarkin always said he had better things to do. After a while Frank stopped mentioning it.

But now Tarkin could think about nothing else. The next day was Friday. Low tide was eight o'clock at night. Tarkin had a strong hunch that's when Magnus Fin was going back under the sea. Fin hadn't been at school that day. All morning Tarkin had worried himself sick thinking Fin had gone off under the sea without even telling him, until someone said he'd been spotted up at the farm.

Friday night. That's when Fin would go. Apart from anything, it would be full moon, which was a magical time in the selkie world. Tarkin also had a hunch a boat would come in handy. He wanted to be a part of this adventure if it was the last thing he did.

People did go fishing at night. Tarkin had seen them, with lights on their boats. So he bit his lip. He twisted his ponytail round and round his fingers. He fiddled with the two silver earrings hooped in his left ear.

Slowly he pushed the door of Frank's shed open and looked down at the floor.

"Um … Frank?"

"Hey, buddy. Good to see you. What can I do for you?"

"Um … know that boat?"

"Sure, Tark. Our boat you mean. What about it?"

"Fancy going, um – fishing – tonight? Buddy?" Tarkin reckoned one evening's practice with Frank would prepare him for taking the boat out alone the next night.

"In the dark? Hey, well … yeah, why not, buddy. Yeah, I've got bait. Got us life jackets an' all. Sure, Tark, and hey, what a great idea. Moonlight fishing, I can't wait!"

Chapter 12

Early the next morning, Fin and Tarkin ran down to the shore. Tarkin was full of his fishing trip: how he had been sick over the side and how Frank hadn't even managed to catch one fish. "Not one! But after spewing up all over Frank's feet I got used to the waves tossing me about. Then I learnt how to use the rudder. It's real easy. Oh man! Frank didn't even know how to hook bait on. You should have seen him. What a loser. He started singing some old-fashioned fishing song. Talk about tuneless?" Tarkin laughed and said he had sailor's legs, just like his dad, but he didn't tell Magnus Fin the real reason for his boat trip.

Magnus Fin felt sorry for Frank. Tarkin was his best friend, there was no doubt about that, but Fin always felt awkward when he started on about Frank.

By this time they had reached the beach. They scuffed up sand and examined the tideline. The tides around full moon always seemed stronger. Full moon, so Fin told Tarkin, was usually when he found his best treasures.

"Look!" Fin yelled, falling to his knees. "A car number plate!"

"Wow! No way – it's from a Ferrari!"

That was another good omen. Now Tarkin needed

to find something too. There were lots of shells, and a few seagull feathers, lots of driftwood, and three plastic bottles, but nothing you could seriously call treasure. Tarkin looked glum. Maybe there was to be no good omen for him … Maybe he'd sink the boat …

"Shuna! Run, hide!"

Tarkin and Magnus Fin looked up. A gull screeched above them, but the sound they'd both heard hadn't been a gull. The boys scrambled to their feet and peered along the beach towards the flat rocks near the cave.

In the distance a girl with very long hair stumbled over the rocks, fell, got up and stumbled again. Fin and Tarkin stared at each other.

"Who's that?" asked Tarkin. Fin shrugged. The girl hadn't seen them. And the way she kept falling looked as though she was in some kind of trouble.

"Come on!" Fin started to run. "Let's see what's wrong."

The two boys tore across the beach, up onto the sandy track and along to where the flat rocks lay like shelves between the land and the sea. They both knew the dead seals were on these rocks. As they came closer they slowed down. The girl had vanished.

The boys scanned the rocks and beach around them. Fin's heart gave a jolt. Another dead seal lay washed up on the ledge. It was like a cemetery for seals. He shivered. Again he heard the voice call, "Shuna – run! Let him go! Quick! We can't stay here." Fin knew that voice. It was coming from behind a rock.

Meanwhile Tarkin was walking towards the dead seals. He had seen something Fin hadn't. Pressed against the body of the fourth seal, almost hidden behind its great round body, lay the girl. Her face was buried deep into the belly of the seal, and she was weeping.

Fin watched, astounded, as Tarkin knelt down beside the girl to comfort her. But when he reached out to gently touch her she screamed and jumped to her feet.

"Miranda!" she yelped. "Help me! It's a human. Oh help!"

In that moment Miranda, her long white hair trailing to her waist, a tangle of dulse for a skirt and a necklace of shells jangling with every step, came out from her hiding place. Seeing his grandmother, Fin ran towards her, but she cried out in distress and quickly stepped back, shaking her head and lifting a hand to ward him off.

"Stop! It has come to me, Fin. Don't approach. The sickness has come to me. Stay back!"

Fin stopped dead in his tracks. Tarkin gazed in amazement. The two long-haired women, dressed in seaweed and shells, seemed to him magical, wonderful creatures. Only once had Tarkin seen such a miraculous sight: the mermaid he'd seen in a freezing lake on a fishing trip with his dad, long ago. Now he blinked, and blinked again, mesmerised.

While Tarkin stared at Shuna, Fin stared at his grandmother. Her snow-white hair covered her face. In one hand she held something – a scallop shell filled with deep-green shreds of seaweed. At her feet lay a pile of fur. Fin looked down at the two seal skins that lay near Miranda's webbed feet. Shuna ran to Miranda and buried her face in the older woman's hair.

"But I want to help," Fin called out. "Please, Miranda – please let me."

But still Miranda shook her head. She placed the scallop shell of seaweed on the sand. Then she slipped her hand into the girl's and bent down. Hurriedly she lifted up the seal skins and ran, pulling the girl with her to the water's edge. The shiny black and grey skin she handed to Shuna. The silvery white one she kept for herself. Seawater now frothed round their white ankles. She looked back at her grandson.

Now Fin could see that the sickness had come. Miranda's eyes, always so bright and clear, were cloudy as though a skin of milk lay over them.

"Let him help, please, Miranda," the young selkie pleaded. "For the memory of my dead brother, let Magnus Fin help us."

"Hush, Shuna, you don't know what you're saying."

"I do. If no one helps it will go on and on and on. Then there'll be no one left to help." Shuna stared at Magnus Fin, her eyes brim-full with tears. "Please?"

"It is my duty to protect you, Magnus Fin," Miranda said, "but if you are set upon this journey, then come, but know that I will do what I can to keep the sickness from you. Take the scallop shell. In it is healing medicine from Neptune. I brought it here, but … I was too late."

Only then did Miranda, flinching, seem to sense there was someone else present. "Tell the human to look away," she said anxiously. "It's not for him to witness shape-shifting."

"Tarkin, close your eyes," Magnus Fin shouted over to his friend.

Tarkin, though, had already heard Miranda and quickly buried his face in his hands. But, as Miranda and Shuna slipped into their seal skins, Tarkin made a tiny gap between two of his fingers, and peered out. He watched as the girl and the woman changed into their seal skins.

It shocked him. It stunned him. The soft white human skin of the women seemed to melt into the thick fur. Their arms became flippers. Their legs knitted together and became one. Then the two beautiful seals, now lying flat on the rocks, hauled their round bodies up to the water's edge then slipped silently into the sea.

"You looked!" Fin gasped, astounded that his best friend would disobey Miranda.

Tarkin said nothing. He could only stare at the place on the rocks where the seals had lain. His face was white. His mouth fell open and his whole body trembled.

"You shouldn't have done that." A tremor of anger shot through Fin's words. "They said not to look. I can't believe you spied on them. You shouldn't have done that, you know."

Still Tarkin was silent. He stumbled to his feet. He opened and closed his mouth, trying to say something. No words came.

"Come on," said Fin, his Ferrari number plate tucked under his arm, and now the scallop shell of precious seaweed held carefully in his hands, "we'd better get to school." He stared strangely at Tarkin and shook his head. "Anybody would think you'd been struck dumb!"

Tarkin opened his mouth. He tried to push out a word, a sound even. But nothing came. Not even a whisper.

Magnus Fin was right. Tarkin had been struck dumb.

Chapter 13

"Wait for me, Tarkin!" Magnus Fin shouted, indicating that he was going to put the Ferrari sign and seaweed in his bedroom and he'd be back out in a flash.

Fin ran into the house, flew up the stairs and into his bedroom, where he slid the number plate and scallop shell under his bed. He grabbed his rucksack then turned and ran downstairs three at a time. He couldn't have been in the house more than a minute, but when he got back outside Tarkin had disappeared.

Fin raced along the track to catch him up. "Tarkin?" he yelled as he ran. "Tarkin, where are you?" But Tarkin must have run like the wind. He was well and truly gone.

Magnus Fin walked up the brae to school alone that morning. Now, as if his planned return under the sea that evening wasn't enough to worry about, there was a missing best friend as well.

"Where's that American pal of yours then?" boomed Mr Sargent when he was marking the register.

This time it was Magnus Fin's turn to shrug his shoulders.

"Off to get a hair cut by any chance? Hmmm?"

"He's got a sore throat, I think," Magnus Fin said, hoping that Tarkin's sudden loss of voice was nothing more sinister than that.

The clock on the classroom wall moved closer and closer to the time of low tide. It was ten o'clock – long division, then two o'clock – French, then half past three.

"Happy St Andrew's day," boomed Mr Sargent as the bell rang and everyone made a quick dash for the door. "And don't forget your maths homework for Monday." But nobody heard that. In seconds the classroom emptied. It was the weekend. Children ran across the playground, cheering and skipping, kicking balls and yelling.

Aquella caught up with her cousin on the way down the brae. "Hey! Where's Tarkin gone?" she asked, out of breath.

"He's got a sore throat," Fin said, without looking her in the eye. Aquella instantly knew something was up. The cousins walked on together, Fin sneaking glances at his watch. Four hours to go. Fin had to be careful what he thought. Aquella could read his mind. But it was hard to control your thoughts. As soon as Fin tried not to think about going under the sea, he thought about going under the sea. Aquella tugged his sleeve.

"You think I'm stupid?"

Fin glanced round at her. "I never said that."

"You really think I don't know?"

Fin played dumb. "Know what?"

"Now you're the stupid one. Know everything! You think I didn't see Shuna? And Miranda? You think I don't know about the sickness? Honestly, Magnus Fin. I've been down to the beach; I've seen the dead seals. Dead selkies if you want to know. You think cos I'm a land girl now I can just turn my back on the sea?"

Fin didn't know what to say. He coughed and looked

down. He didn't know she felt homesick. She seemed happy. She was in a girl's band. She had friends. Sarah and Kayla hung about with her. Everybody seemed to love Aquella. She was kind and gentle and popular. But as she stared at Magnus Fin her green eyes blazed. She wasn't so gentle now.

"You think I like being left out? You think I can just crawl out of the sea and forget about my whole life and family and friends? Oh, Fin, I cry myself to sleep. I miss the sea so much. Sometimes I think I'll never get used to squeezing my feet into shoes and eating vegetables. And now the sickness has come to them and there's nothing I can do about it, because if I get salt water on my skin I'll shrivel up." By this time large tears were rolling down Aquella's face.

Fin knew about the skin thing. Skin was important for selkies. Aquella had to go a year and a day on dry land, without so much as a splash of seawater, for her skin to fully adapt to air. Fin laid a hand on her shoulder for comfort.

They had reached the track now that led to the cottage. Both of them stared out over the water. "Mostly I close my eyes so I don't see the sea. Sometimes I even put my hands over my ears so I don't hear it. I'm afraid I might wake up in the middle of the night and just go – back into the sea."

Magnus Fin patted her back. He felt like crying himself. He had no idea it was so hard for her. Poor Aquella. She looked at him, wiping her tears with her long black hair. "But I stay, Fin. I stay because it's good to be a land girl. And I stay because I wouldn't be good to anyone shrivelled up." She managed a tiny smile.

71

"But at least tell me what you're going to do, what you're planning. I know I'm a selkie without a skin, but maybe I can do *something*."

Fin glanced again at his watch then at Aquella. "I'm going under the sea at eight o'clock tonight. I've got a present for Miranda that might help. It's my last baby tooth. And there's something hidden behind a weird rock. I want to see what it is. Maybe I can do something to help. Maybe I can't. But I have to try." Just blurting these words out gave Fin a feeling of strength. And it felt good to have someone to talk to.

"I'll come down to the beach tonight," Aquella said. She had stopped crying now and seemed excited. "When you're under the sea send messages to me with your thoughts. If there's anything I can do tell me. Please, Fin – I need to help them. You understand that, don't you?"

Fin nodded. "Promise you won't get salt water on your skin?"

Aquella smiled. "Not a drop, I promise."

Then Fin, suddenly remembering, said, "Tarkin's lost his voice. He watched Miranda and Shuna change into their seal skins. That's why he skipped school. He can't speak."

"Oh no!" Aquella threw her hands to her face. "Why did he go and do that?"

But Fin didn't answer because just then Barbara appeared at the front door of the cottage. "Hey! I got you two presents," she called, waving for them both to come in. "Something nice to wear for the ceilidh tonight."

"Ceilidh? Oh crikey, I totally forgot about the ceilidh," Magnus Fin said to Aquella while waving to his mother.

"I've got a kilt for you, Magnus, and a beautiful green dress for you, Aquella." Barbara was waving for them to come and try the new clothes on.

"Little does she know," Aquella whispered, nudging her cousin in the ribs, "you'll be swimming in a wetsuit deep under the sea. Some kilt! Some ceilidh!"

"And I thought we should maybe practise a few ceilidh dances," Barbara said as the two children stepped into the cottage. "It'll be Aquella's first ceilidh. Now isn't that exciting?"

Barbara beamed at the children while Aquella laughed nervously and Magnus Fin coughed and almost choked. "Yeah!" they chorused, flashing a baffled look at each other.

Barbara put fiddle music on and the sound wafted into the garden, drifted over the stone wall, glided down the beach and danced out to sea.

Chapter 14

Meanwhile up in the croft at the edge of the village, Tarkin was lying in bed refusing to speak to anyone. His mother insisted on coming into his room every half hour to check on him. "At least write to me, honey, if that makes things easier on your throat."

Tarkin shook his head. Why wouldn't she just leave him alone? And then, as if her frequent "feeling any better honey?" calls, and trays piled with bagels and cream cheese, and glasses of warm milk weren't enough, Frank insisted on sitting on the edge of his bed telling him stories.

"There was this tortoise and it got racing with a hare. At least, I think it was a hare …"

Tarkin closed his eyes and sunk down under the duvet.

"Course you'd think any day the hare's gonna beat the tortoise, wouldn't you? Well, not so …"

Tarkin was so miserable he wanted to cry, but he sure wasn't going to cry in front of Frank. These selkies had put a curse on him; he knew it. This was no simple sore throat. His throat felt fine. Why oh why did he peep?

"So this tortoise, the thing is, he just kept plodding on. That's the secret you see, you just keep on going. You don't stop."

Then Frank got up and left. As soon as the door closed, Tarkin pulled down the duvet so that he could breathe. He had the first grateful thought he'd had for hours. It came to him slowly and made him feel just a tiny bit better.

Well, at least I can breathe. Then that thought led to another, which made him feel even better. *And at least I can think.* Then he pulled back the duvet and swung his legs out of bed. He stood up and walked over to the window. *And at least I can walk.*

It may have had something to do with the tortoise who kept on going, but Tarkin suddenly felt a whole lot better. He could breathe, think and walk. He studied the sky. The afternoon light was already fading. He had missed a whole day at school.

He got busy, pulling his rain trousers and life jacket out of the cupboard. According to his moon-phase calendar, low tide was in four hours time. He didn't want to miss that. He needed Frank and his mother out of the way. He grabbed a sheet of paper and quickly wrote:

Kaylay on in village hall. You should go. You'll meet people and Fin says it's great. I am OK. Tarkin.

As for steering a boat, there was nothing to it. Tarkin had seen where Frank left the key for the starting motor. It was hanging up on a nail in his shed. And the shed was unlocked. If Fin got into trouble Tarkin would be right there on the sea, with a blanket, and sweets, and a torch. And even if it was a bit scary out alone on the dark ocean, Fin would only be gone a few minutes in human time. Tarkin was zingy with excitement now.

He was going to be in on this adventure. He wasn't just going to sit on a rock chanting and eating toffee. Oh no. He was going to take a boat out to sea and help the selkies – even if they did put a curse on him.

He posted his note through the living-room door then jumped back into bed.

"What a good idea, honey," his mother said two minutes later, waving his note.

"Wanna come with us, buddy?" asked Frank. The adults stood together, framed in Tarkin's bedroom doorway, smiling anxiously.

Tarkin shook his head and pointed to his throat.

"He needs to rest, Frank," said Martha gently. "A sick boy can't dance."

Tarkin nodded vigorously and pointed to the pillow.

"But we can't leave him on his own," said Frank.

Tarkin folded his hands under his cheek, meaning he'd be fast asleep. Then he pointed down to the village, meaning they should go there and dance.

"I'll ask Rena next door to keep an eye on you, honey," Martha said. Then she kissed Tarkin, ruffled his hair and left him. He could hear them in the hallway discussing what they'd wear.

"Think I'll wear my plaid pants," said Frank.

"I'll wear my kilt," said Martha.

And I'll wear a life jacket, thought Tarkin, as darkness fell and the moon slowly rose over the water.

Chapter 15

"Magnus and Aquella are coming with us to the ceilidh. Don't they look lovely?"

Ragnor nodded. They did.

"Thing is, Barbara," said Aquella, after doing a twirl in her new green dress, "we just need to visit Tarkin first. He's not well. Then we'll come as soon as we can." This was not strictly a lie and Aquella smiled her sweetest smile. Fin nodded in agreement.

Ragnor flashed him an anxious look. *Remember to heed your instinct, son.*

Fin glanced at his father and nodded. "You look grand in a kilt," his father said, and winked.

Magnus Fin ate three helpings of shepherd's pie. He'd read how food is converted into warmth and energy. He'd need warmth. He'd need energy. It was the last day of November. No one swam in the sea in the north of Scotland on the last day of November. He munched on.

"Tuck in, son," said Barbara, "you'll need lots of energy for dancing."

Ragnor, chewing slowly, looked at his son. "Aye, Fin, you'll need lots of energy right enough. Tuck in."

After supper Magnus Fin lay on his bed, so stuffed he couldn't move. He had to loosen the buckle on his kilt. He could hear Aquella downstairs. She was doing Barbara's hair and chatting. Ragnor was doing the dishes. Fin felt so full he was sure he would jump into the sea and immediately sink. For the hundredth time he glanced at his watch. Half an hour to go.

Fin could hear sounds drifting up from the living room. His parents were going for a drink before the ceilidh. They were putting coats on and laughing, calling up to him to send their love to Tarkin and see you later at the dance. The front door opened then closed. He heard their footsteps on the path. He heard their voices on the wind, like chattering starlings. Then they were gone.

In seconds Aquella was at his bedroom door. He was so full of shepherd's pie the only thing he wanted to do was sleep.

"Right, Fin! Quick! Get ready!" Aquella commanded, her voice trembling with excitement. "I've put Neptune's seaweed into this locket with your baby tooth. Put it on, quick." Fin rubbed his belly and groaned.

"But what about Tarkin?" he asked, still lying in bed and beginning to feel sick, as Aquella snapped the locket shut.

"What about him?"

"He said he wanted to help. He said he would be there."

"Well, maybe he's there already. If not, we haven't got time to fetch him. Come on, Magnus Fin. Get up! And here," she added, flinging him a pair of swimming goggles, "these might come in handy for the stinging brown gunge. Put them round your neck. Now come on!"

Fin groaned again. He rubbed his belly then looked at his watch. Aquella was right. It was time to wriggle into his wetsuit.

"Might be a good idea to take the kilt off," Aquella said, laughing, "and I promise," she added, clapping her hands over her eyes, "I won't look."

At quarter to eight Magnus Fin and Aquella left the cottage, he in his wetsuit, she in her green dress with a pink puffy jacket on top, and a hat and gloves and scarf. The moon was now up and a silver path lay over the sea. It was almost light outside in an eerie colourless way.

They ran along the beach path, Fin casting his eyes around for a glimpse of Tarkin. Maybe he was on the black rock waiting? Maybe he had brought a flask of hot chocolate?

But as they neared the skerries there was no sign of Tarkin. The only things on the rocks were the letters M F. The white writing screamed at him. Fin clutched at his moon-stone and ran on, glad for the company of his cousin. But soon, he knew, they'd come to salt water. Then he'd be on his own.

"You have three minutes, Fin," she said when they reached the skerries. She squeezed his arm and smiled encouragingly. "Take your trainers off. I'll look after them until you come back. I'll be in Ragnor's cave. Good luck."

Ragnor's cave was close to the flat rocks where the dead seals lay. The same place he had seen Miranda and Shuna. It was a special place for the selkies; Fin knew that. He looked at Aquella anxiously as he handed her his shoes.

"I'll be fine," she said, "and remember – if you

need help let me know. I'll be waiting. I'll be the land lookout. Now go!"

She ran across the beach. The tide was far out so the salt water wouldn't touch her. Fin watched her slow down. In the moonlight he saw her stand close to the dead seals then she turned and waved him on. He had one minute. He jumped over the skerries and headed for the black rock.

Fin leapt from rock to rock. Panting hard, he hoisted himself up onto the black rock and curled his webbed feet over the ledge. There was no one to count for him this time.

"Ten, nine, eight ..." he shouted out loud. The moonlight shone bright. He gazed down at the water. It glinted like silver. He heard a thrumming noise. Thinking it was the churning of the water below he shouted on, "Seven, six, five ..."

The rumbling noise grew louder. Someone's thoughts dived into his. *Four, three, two ...*

Fin glanced up. In the distance he saw a small boat. A torchlight from it flashed towards him: on, off, on, off. That was Tarkin's signal! And those were Tarkin's thoughts. His best friend was heading towards him – in a boat!

One – JUMP!

Magnus Fin grinned. He waved. The torchlight flashed back.

Then he jumped.

Chapter 16

Magnus Fin hit the water with a loud splash. It was freezing! Gasping with the shock, he clutched at the mother-of-pearl handle and pulled. The rock door to the selkie world opened. From the crack between the worlds the emerald-green light flashed – and he was through.

But through to what? Where was the crab? The water churned around him, twisting him in a spinning vortex, its force sucking him down. Magnus Fin was in a whirlpool. It pulled at him and spun him. Everything was a blur. Booming sounds near deafened him. The brilliant light near blinded him. His lungs felt fit to burst. He floundered with his arms and legs, helpless in this tube of whirling water. Had he jumped straight into a sea storm?

Just when he was sure he would faint, the churning, spinning and whirling motions ceased. He was thrown forward by a tidal force. One more booming sound and instantly the water calmed. Everything grew still and quiet. Eerily quiet. Or had Magnus Fin gone deaf?

Fin ventured forward. His arms trembled but he managed slowly to swim. He glanced above. He glanced below. With the silver beam of his torch eye-lights he scanned the dark seawater. What strange world was this? No swaying arms of seaweed moved. No fish swam. No crab was here to guide him. Nothing!

Nothing, that was, except for a few slow swaying seals, sleeping peacefully. Thankful he wasn't alone, Fin nudged the seals, but try as he might, and he did, nothing would wake them. Confused, Fin left them to their dreams and swam on through the dark silent water.

After a few strokes he bumped against something. Feeling forward, his hands came up against what felt like metal. Panicking, he swam back, but only a few strokes. Again he met the same resistance. Where was he? Frantic now, he swam up. He swam down. He swam to the sides again, kicking his legs furiously through the water. Then he stopped and slumped against the wall. There was nowhere to go. He was in some kind of container, a sunken ship perhaps. And unless he was mistaken, there was no way out.

He wanted to scream for help. But he'd only been under the water for minutes, seconds even. He couldn't call for Aquella already, surely? He wanted to protect her, and he wanted her to think he was brave and strong.

What about Tarkin then? Hadn't Tarkin's thoughts come to him and told him to jump? Perhaps he really was close by somewhere in a boat. Tarkin had lost his voice – but now, just maybe, he had discovered thought transmission.

Fin concentrated hard on Tarkin. He tried to picture him. Then he tried to send his thoughts towards him: *HELP ME! I'm stuck in a sunken ship. Oh help!*

But after a few seconds the thoughts bounced back: *HELP ME! I'm stuck in a sunken ship.* Fin groaned. The ship, or whatever it was, was sound proof – and thought proof. *Oh help!*

Magnus Fin didn't cry very often. But he cried then, and floated helplessly round and round in the silent prison filled with briny water, a few blissfully unconscious seals and his own salt tears.

Chapter 17

Tarkin was glad that the village hall was surrounded by pine trees. So even if Frank did step outside for some fresh air he wouldn't see his fishing boat churning across the moonlit ocean. When Tarkin cut the engine and let the boat drift on the smooth sea he caught snatches of music on the wind. He grinned. If only his dad could see him now. He couldn't believe how easy it had been to steer the boat out of the harbour, and now, how well he was managing. He was probably a natural born seafarer. Hadn't his dad spent a couple of years in the United States Marine Corp? Seafaring was in the blood.

Tarkin, with his hand gently on the rudder, let the boat drift, trying more or less to keep the rock where Fin jumped off in his sight. The full moon flooded the beach, the coast and the sea with a pale silvery glow.

Tarkin checked his watch. It was one of those watches that lit up. Magnus Fin, so his watch informed him, had been gone all of one minute. From what Fin had told him, a minute on land could feel like a day underwater – so in sea time, Fin had been gone a long time. Tarkin scanned his torch across the water but there was no sign of him, so Tarkin tore the wrapper off a toffee and ate it.

Maybe it was the toffee, though more probably the

swell that gently rocked the boat, but Tarkin felt his stomach lurch. Under his unsteady feet the boat rocked like a cradle. Tarkin snatched in air, and wound his fingers tightly over the edge of the boat. He groaned. The last thing he wanted was to be sick.

Frank's words of advice from the night before came back to him, "Bend your knees and go with the flow, buddy." Tarkin bent his knees and moved with the gentle rocking motion of the boat. It helped. He breathed out and unclenched his grip.

Seasickness scare over, Tarkin checked again that everything was in place: towel, life jacket, rope, huge bag of sweets, blanket, torch, pen and paper. The water slapped against the hull of the boat. The moon shone. Tarkin sat at the stern guiding the boat through the calm water and chewing his toffee.

Awesome! Life at sea, he thought, *is definitely the life for me. What muckle bliss.*

Aquella sat on the flat rock, with four dead seals for company. She knew these seals, had swum with them, and at solstice times had come ashore with them. Fin had gone, into the freezing water. And there, if she wasn't mistaken, in a small fishing boat out at sea, was Tarkin. She couldn't see anyone with him. Her strong selkie eyesight could only make out Tarkin wearing a bulky life jacket. She felt relieved seeing the life jacket but nervous at the thought of what an eleven-year-old boy in a boat alone, at night – who didn't know how to swim – might get up to.

"Oh, Tarkin," she sighed, standing to see him better, "in the name of Neptune, don't try anything heroic."

Aquella liked Tarkin fine. She could see how he admired Fin. He had even tried once to wear a coloured contact lens so he too would have different coloured eyes. And he was forever speaking about the mermaid he once saw. He wanted adventure badly. More than anything he wanted to be different. And there was Magnus Fin, as different as day is to night, adventure seeming to seek him out, and him wishing he could be normal.

Aquella watched the little boat. It seemed to bob about aimlessly. It was enough that she was there to help Fin if he got into trouble. Tarkin was bound to be more a hindrance than a help.

"Tarkin!" she shouted. But he was further away than he seemed and she didn't dare go any closer for fear of salt water. "Tarkin don't be stupid!" But her words evaporated into the night air. "Now I've got you to look out for as well as Magnus Fin," she said to herself, annoyed that a boy who couldn't even swim would take a boat out.

Aquella stood on the rocks and waited, for what she didn't know. She stared out to sea, resisting the urge to walk right into it. She thought about how Ragnor had said the best way to be a land girl was not to think too much about her life under the sea.

"It's like Tarkin," Ragnor had said to her, comforting her one night when she felt homesick. He'd been listening while she struggled on with her reading, and when she gave up he just sat with her.

"How?" she'd asked, not understanding how she was like Tarkin. She had black hair, he had blond hair – she had green eyes, he had blue eyes – he was skinny, she wasn't. And now – she was responsible – and he wasn't.

"Well, he probably misses America," Ragnor said. "I know he misses his dad. But he's in Scotland now. Here – up in the north – same as you – and he's getting on with it. Think of it like living in another country. It helps. And it doesn't help to think too much about the past, Aquella."

That made sense to Aquella. She was a foreigner in a new land. And she was determined to make the most of it, just like Magnus Fin's friend from America. She had looked at Tarkin differently after that. He, like her, had also come from far away.

And he, like her, just wanted to help. Thinking this, she breathed in the salty tang of the sea, sat back down on the flat rocks, pulled her jacket about her, and waited.

Chapter 18

Magnus Fin didn't know how long he had been in this prison. He wasn't hungry – though the shepherd's pie may have had something to do with that. He wasn't even thirsty. He was bored. And bored was the last thing he expected to be in the selkie world. He was also – he could feel it pulsing inside him like a slow-boiling kettle – angry.

HELP! LET ME OUT! But it only took seconds for the thoughts to echo back: *HELP! LET ME OUT!*

Fin hammered his fists on the steel walls, which, Fin discovered as he hammered, sloped up to a point. He was surely in an upturned sunken ship, or a tanker. He kicked as hard as he could, but no one heard him. Fin howled. He punched. But the steel was hard, his fellow prisoners were still asleep, and his fist throbbed.

HELP!

HELP!

It's Magnus Fin, son of Ragnor.

It's Magnus Fin, son of Ragnor.

It's me – M F.

It's me – M F.

Don't leave me alone.

You are not alone.

Fin swung round. A slamming sound boomed in his ears. The water churned then grew instantly calm again.

You are not alone. It came again and it wasn't his thoughts. Hope filled him. Eagerly Fin scanned his prison.

Swimming towards him was a black and silver seal. She swam up to Magnus Fin and nuzzled him gently. *It is for the sake of our health.*

Fin stared into the warm dark eyes of the seal. A flicker of recognition stirred in him.

The seal nodded. *Aye, Fin, it is Shuna. I begged you to help us on the beach, but Miranda is afraid. She wants to protect us. The sickness will not come into this sealed place, or so they hope. The bay near here was always special to us selkies, not least because you, Ragnor and now Aquella live close by. But, Fin, the selkies are dying there. Their eyesight is failing. Bones are breaking and even the young are fainting and falling. Locked up like this we are safe. Until it passes. That is what Miranda says. We, the selkies who are still healthy, must stay here until it passes.*

Fin stared at her, not understanding. *Until what passes?*

The sickness. We selkies have to be careful with our skin, you know that Fin.

Fin circled around the young seal. He didn't intend to be locked up in this sunken ship until the sickness, whatever it was, passed. He had not jumped into the sea and pushed open the rock door to the selkie world for this. He had to help his grandmother.

It won't come to me. I'm half human, remember? It won't come to me. Fin wasn't so sure but he tried to sound confident. *You asked me to come and help. The crab wants me to help. I know he does. And Miranda, the one I want to help, has kept me prisoner. There must be a way out of here, Shuna. Help me to escape. I can stop this sickness. I know I can. And I'm not so sure it's a sickness anyway.*

Shuna stared into Magnus Fin's eyes. *Of course it is. It killed many of our kind before.*

But I saw the green staring eye, and the stinking gunge. I think someone or something is poisoning the selkies – some menacing creature with a wild green eye. I saw it. Fin lifted the locket around his neck to show Shuna. *And I've got my last milk tooth in here, and Neptune's seaweed. They can help. Now I've got to get out of here. Help me, Shuna.*

Shuna glanced at the other selkies. Some of them had woken up and were now swimming towards the human child, curiosity wide in their eyes.

The only way out of here is if another selkie is brought in. That's the only chance. Any seals found whose eyes have not turned white are brought to this place.

What is this place anyway?

One of your steel ships. It's upside down. There is one tiny porthole blocked with a stone. When a healthy seal is found the nurse seals remove the stone and push the healthy seal in here. What do you call it – quarantine? To have any chance of escape you must wait by the porthole. As soon as it opens, Fin, slip out – quick as an eel. I'll make a banging noise to distract them.

They? Who are they?

The helper seals. The nurses, I told you. But the ones that brought me here were half blind themselves. Escape might be easier that you think. They will hardly be able to see you. But it's not the helper seals you need fear. It's the sickness you should fear. It killed my brother.

The other seals had gathered round now. They seemed to be nodding and, with their mournful eyes, wishing him well.

Fin didn't waste a second. The stone over the porthole could open at any moment. He stroked Shuna's sleek face then swam quickly over to the round steel porthole. He tried to kick the stone away but it was wedged in tight. All healthy selkie eyes were on him now. He hovered by the porthole, treading water to keep him from floating upwards.

May Neptune guide you, Shuna called out.

Where is he anyway? Magnus Fin asked from his place by the porthole.

Far away, Shuna told him, *far, far away where the oil clings to the water.*

Fin shuddered. The great king of the sea, Neptune, would not be able to help him. He had other work to do. Feeling more alone than ever, Magnus Fin clutched his moon-stone and waited.

And he waited. Shuna had fallen asleep. Peacefully she floated about in the quarantined tanker. Fin couldn't imagine what loud distracting noises she would be able to make, floating about in the land of nod.

Magnus Fin felt tired himself. His chin rolled down against his chest. His eyelids grew heavy. Oh, to sleep for a day, a week, eternity. He closed his eyes, stopped treading water and floated up through the upturned hull.

Wake up, Fin. It's opening.

Fin shook himself. He blinked and rubbed his eyes. Shuna was thudding her tail fin against the side of the ship, to and fro, to and fro. The porthole, with a thundering grinding noise, was opening.

Now, Fin. Go! And Neptune go with you!

The helper seals called for Shuna to calm herself. The stone was fully pulled back now. The waters churned and frothed. Fin spied the gap. He saw a seal being flung into the hull. With not a second to lose Fin dived. He squirmed through the narrowing gap in the porthole, scraping his foot as it closed, stubbing his toe. Just in the nick of time he yanked his foot free as the stone crashed back into the porthole behind him.

He dived deep, on and away through the water. His heart was a drum in his chest. His big toe throbbed. *Thank Neptune,* he cried, *I'm freeeeee!*

Through forests of kelp and algae he swam. Through rocky caverns he swam. *I'm coming, Miranda!* he called loudly in his thoughts. *I'm bringing the medicine!* But not a murmur came in reply.

Plunging onwards, thoughts of his beautiful, brave and ailing grandmother fuelled his every stroke. With jellyfish, darting eels and then salmon he swam. He needed to find the canyon. He had to find the weeping rock. The image of the green eye haunted him. The sickness wasn't invisible. It had a grotesque staring eye and Fin was going to find it.

Chapter 19

In the village hall, the St Andrew's ceilidh had begun. Tam was there on the accordion and Johnny on the fiddle, tuning up. Jeanette was passing round sausage rolls and Wendy and Francis were welcoming the newcomers, Frank and Martha from America.

Out at sea, Frank's fishing boat was about to run out of diesel. Not that Frank had any inkling of that. Nor did the boat's skipper, Tarkin.

On the flat rocks by the cave, Aquella was struggling to stay awake. It had been so long since she had been this close to the sea. The swish of the waves breaking over the skerries soothed her. The tang of the salt sea that she so often dreamt of filled her lungs. She hadn't been this close to home for months. She felt more relaxed than she had ever felt as a land girl. In front of her the waves lapped, running up the stony shore then rippling back. Up and back, up and back. Aquella, eyelids drooping, kicked off her uncomfortable human shoes, bunched a tangle of seaweed into a pillow, laid her head down upon it then closed her eyes and slept.

Deep under the sea, swimming in wide strokes through twisting caverns and over ribbed plains, Magnus Fin had never felt stronger. He was in deep water now. He could feel the weight with every stroke. When he needed to rest he treaded water. Below him, on the seabed, blue lobsters scavenged on a rotting shark. Fin shivered and kicked his webbed feet.

Through wide basins teeming with fish he swam, grateful that the many weird and wonderful marine creatures, though curious, didn't seem interested in making a boy in a wetsuit their next feast.

A huge octopus with long tentacles swirled upwards and brushed his cheek. The longest worm he'd ever seen, like a writhing giant's bootlace, looped around Fin's foot, then recoiled and slunk off. Bright, round sea urchins lay in their thousands on a carpet of red and green seaweed, and dead man's fingers waved as he glided by.

He had met no seals yet; slithering darting eels, huge shoals of glistening salmon, trembling luminescent jellyfish, he'd even heard the deep bass song of a whale, but seals were nowhere to be found.

Seals would have been good company, but the lack of them made Fin focus on the mission ahead. It was a green staring eye he was searching for, weeping brown oozing tears. He needed to find the crack in the rock and somehow put a stop to this poisonous creature, then quickly find Miranda and give her the medicine. *Somehow.*

Fin glided above the ghostly remains of a sunken ship wondering, *How?*

He followed a shoal of glittering herring. Biting his lip he had to admit to himself, he had *no* idea how he was supposed to put a stop to this poisonous creature. There was something about that eye that turned his spine to butter. But he, Magnus Fin, had defeated a great monster, hadn't he?

At that moment a jellyfish brushed his face. Fin winced and pushed it away.

Miranda! he called, but only the sound of waves booming against rocky caverns called back to him. *Miranda!*

It was then the terrible thought hit him that maybe he was too late. What if Miranda was dead? Panic rushed through him. The great Neptune was far away. And where was Miranda? Fin felt like the tiniest boy in the deepest ocean. And, he realised as his panic grew, this tiny boy was lost.

The ocean seemed fathomless. There were so many dark caverns, so many forests of kelp. It all looked the same. Should he turn right? Or left? Frantically he glanced around. Which way now? He twisted round in the water.

Where are you? he called to any selkies that might hear him. Even a fish might show him where to go. *Don't leave me alone!*

The deep silence of the sea was the only reply.

The sea that only moments before had seemed friendly and exciting was suddenly menacing. The swaying seaweed and plankton were now tantalising witchy fingers out to get him. Under his wetsuit a trickle of sweat ran down his spine. Which way should he go? Back the way he came? Or even deeper down through the dark sea? He grabbed his moon-stone.

Instinct! The word flashed into his mind. "If you're lost, follow it, son." That's what his dad had said. "Selkies have a kind of marine radar, like a compass.

It's in our nose, it's in our belly. It tells us the way to go."

Fin clapped his hand on his belly. His dad was right. Instantly Magnus Fin knew where to go. The panic left him. He twisted his body to the left and swam on, deeper.

In the immensity of the ocean one green eye was a pin-prick, but suddenly Fin was following a map in his mind. He *would* find it, *and* the cause of this sickness. As he swam he remembered the underwater cities Sargent had mentioned in school. He scanned the dark waters beneath him. He saw sea anemones, kelp and waving fronds of bladderwrack, but no sunken city. No glimpse of Atlantis. Only rocks, studded with mussels, barnacles, limpets and cockles. But a rock, Fin reminded himself, was what he was seeking.

Fin dived deeper to examine the rocks. One in particular beckoned him, a small dark rock that stood alone, wedged into sand and sludge. Fin swam closer. His heart skipped a beat. Upon that rock, in silvery wavy writing, the letters M F stared up at him.

Fin slapped his hand on his belly but could only feel the thudding of his heart. *Hey!* he shouted out in his underwater thoughts. *I'm here to help. I came! I'm here to help the selkies. I've brought medicine. Hey! M F, that's me. Is there anybody there?*

Nothing answered. Only a faint thudding sound, as though someone, or something, far in the distance, was thumping a battering ram against a rock door.

Chapter 20

Hey, dude! What's with the human?

Little diver gone and got himself good and lost, looks like to me.

And me.

No wrecks here, diver boy, just us dudes.

Fin was surrounded. He twisted round but they had him covered.

Diver boy looks discombobulated, dontcha think, guv?

That's the word, Spike. Or dontcha mean dislocated? Ha ha. Will be soon!

The gang of fish swam closer. Teeth flashing. Wide mouths pulsing. Rusted hooks hanging from festering lips. Faces puffing up. Eyes blinking.

Fin gulped. There was only one course of action – politeness.

Pleased to meet you, said Fin. *So, um, how are you all doing?*

The gang leader glided even closer – so close its sharp white teeth came into biting range. Magnus Fin could see these teeth had been in some scrapes. Most were crooked and broken and rotten. And half of them weren't sharp or white at all. Fin could see a whole sorry life story in this set of teeth, to say nothing of the rusted fish hooks festering away in its lips. One fish hook stuck out from the ugly fish's face.

Don't suppose you have dentists down here? Fin asked.

The gang leader chattered its teeth. They sounded like castanets. The other hoodlums laughed.

Think he taste good? Spike, the teeth-snapper said, slobbering.

Bit thin, boss. Bit scrawny. Them divers are always rubbery and thin.

Politeness didn't seem to be working. The gang looked hungry. They circled him menacingly, fin tails swishing, slapping Magnus Fin in the face. *So what are you doing here?* Fin asked, trying to protect his face with his hands.

We're just cruising. We're hanging loose. Just loafing around. Fin got the idea. *We're just seeking amusement.*

Fin groaned and put his hand on his belly. They weren't so clever, these fish. If politeness wasn't going to get him out of this scrape, wit would have to.

Seen any more divers around here? Fin asked the big boss, the one with the hook in his face.

Big boss sneered. Those puffy, wounded lips parted. Fin shrank back, wondering – was this a fish smile?

Yes, big fellows? Huge shoulders? Fin went on. *They were here a second ago.*

Big fellows, you say?

Huge. Enormous. Really fat.

Which way they go, shrimp face?

Yeah, you tell us or we'll eat you and spit you out! That was the scaly sidekick, who had so many hooks stuck in his mouth he seemed to have a metal beard.

For a second Magnus Fin thought about his escape from the sunken ship. That was nothing compared to the amount of escapes this gang had been through.

The fat guy went that way, said Fin, pointing into a deep kelp forest. *He's probably hiding in the fronds.*

As quickly as they had appeared, the gang of ragged hungry fish flicked round and headed for the forest.

Magnus Fin was ready to swim away fast when underneath him a clam shell opened, and out scuttled the little crab. It darted round behind a rock, and Fin, not knowing what else to do, dived in next to him. The rock was big enough to hide behind. Magnus Fin hunched down close to the crab.

You just wait here till the coast is clear, said the crab.

Fin could feel the tickly prickly movement of the crab crawling up his arm and coming to rest on his shoulder. Fin adjusted his eye-lights by blinking and let a soft glow fall upon the small pink creature with the tiny red eyes.

So M F, it said, *what took you so long?*

Look, said Fin, *I hope you don't mind me asking but – who are you exactly?*

The crab clicked his pincers together and seemed to consider Fin's question. *Let's just say I work for the boss.*

The boss? Who exactly was the boss? And though Fin had barely thought the thought, the crab was quick to answer.

The Big N.

The Big N. Who's that? A newt? A nurse shark? A narwhale?

Come on, Magnus Fin. Get that brain in gear. You'll need it for the job ahead.

But what job? I don't understand.

How about less talk and more action … And with that, the crab was gone, away from their hiding place and scuttling through the water at a rate of knots.

Fin kicked his legs and swam. Once again he found himself following this mysterious crab. *And who,* Fin shuddered as he swam in fast wide strokes through the water, *or what, is the Big N?* Suddenly it dawned on him. He swam faster.

Hey! Crab! Do you mean Neptune?

The crab stopped scuttling and swung round, its red eyes flashing through the dark water. *Congratulations, M F – you got it!*

This underwater adventure seemed to be taking longer than usual. Tarkin looked at his watch and felt the first quiver of anxiety. Magnus Fin had been gone four minutes. That had been three toffees and a swig of orange juice. Tarkin thanked his lucky stars for a calm sea and a bright moon – and for the circle of pine trees around the village hall. Apart from one fleeting jab of seasickness he felt fine. Yes, the calm seafaring life was definitely for him. He didn't much fancy being tossed about on a choppy ocean with the rain coming at him sideways and sharks hovering nearby.

Sharks! Drat! He tried to push the thought away, tried to picture happy looking dolphins and gentle kind-eyed seals. Why did he have to go and think of sharks? Now he couldn't get them out of his mind: tiger sharks, great white sharks, basking sharks, bull sharks. They grew enormous. They glided through the infested water to theme tunes and circled his tiny fishing boat. Reef sharks, goblin sharks, lemon sharks. He stuffed another toffee into his mouth and chewed furiously. He peered longingly into the water. *Fin!* he thought. *Buddy! Where are you?*

He looked up. In the distance he could make out dark shapes of rocks and cliffs. Tarkin chewed his lip. If he wasn't mistaken, land was further away than he thought. Although the sea seemed still as a millpond there must, Tarkin reckoned, be some movement or swell to it. In four minutes of drifting Tarkin had travelled a fair distance out to sea. His worry level rose. He swallowed the toffee, gulped noiselessly and stood up fast, making the boat rock like a cradle. He staggered over to the outboard motor and turned the key.

The small engine puttered, spluttered, coughed out a dark puff of smoke and died.

Tarkin would have screamed if he'd had a voice to scream with. Here he was, the captain of the rescue vessel, and now it was he who needed rescuing. He whimpered soundlessly and his body shook like a leaf. Towel, torch, sweets, rope and blanket weren't much good now.

That's when his foot bumped up against something. He knelt down and fumbled at his feet. If he could have, he would have shouted for joy because he had just found the oars. It had been a long time since he and his dad had taken a rowing boat out on the lake in Canada. But Tarkin remembered what to do. "Put your back into it, son," that's what his dad had told him.

Quickly he got to work, hauling up the heavy oars and linking them into the round oarlocks on either side of the boat. Panting hard, he managed to secure the oars. He had seen rowers on the television. They never looked where they were going. It seemed dangerous but Tarkin reckoned these strong men on the television probably knew more about rowing than he did.

So Tarkin sat down facing out to sea. He dipped the oars into the water and pulled. It was hard work. He put his back into it. The water dragged at the oars. Tarkin heaved them through the water for all he was worth. Was the boat moving? He hoped so. He kept rowing.

At least he had forgotten the sharks!

Chapter 21

For one so tiny, the crab swam fast. Fin followed, clutching his moon-stone. He had a strong feeling that the green eye he was seeking was close by. He would need every ounce of courage he could summon. The fish gang had been bad enough. Magnus Fin shot a few glances behind to check that he'd lost them. He caught up with the crab and as they darted through the water Fin tried to make conversation.

That ugly fish gang must have had more escapes than I've had hot dinners, he said, shuddering at the memory of the festering sores and rusting fish hooks. *They must be really strong to wrench themselves away from fishing lines.*

The crab's thoughts travelled swift and clear. *Strong? Those bullies aren't strong. They range the seas looking for weaker creatures to bully. No, they're not strong. Fishermen just saw how ugly they were and threw them right back. I don't blame them. Now, where is it?*

Where's what?

The canyon. Ah yes, this way. Come on, quick.

You're not going to disappear again, are you? Magnus Fin asked, somehow knowing what the answer would be. *It would make me feel better knowing you're around.*

Don't worry, I'll be around. I'm always around. You know, even if I vanish from time to time, I'm still around. Oh, and

103

don't worry about the bullies, said the crab. *If they come back just threaten to pull their fish hooks. That'll send the fear of a tsunami into them. Right, here we are. A job for you. Are you feeling strong, M F?*

Um, crab ... what job am I supposed to do?

The crab fixed Magnus Fin with his piercing red eyes. This, Fin could tell, was serious. *The boss is away on another job. Miranda is working flat out to save her people. Listen well – Neptune told me to call on you. You have the combined power of land and sea. And you've already proved yourself a hero for us. Something behind this rock is poisoning the sea. The selkies are dying, Fin.*

Fin stared at the crab. He felt a lump rise in his throat. Neptune, the great sea king, had asked for his help?

Crab, Fin said, finding his voice, *I think there's another monster behind this illness. It has a scary green eye. I know – I've seen it.*

Well, now's the time to go and put a stop to it, the crab said, adding, as Magnus Fin knew he would, *cos this is where you and I bid each other bye-bye. Good luck, M F. I'll never be far away. So long.*

And with that the crab disappeared.

Magnus Fin didn't ask where he was supposed to go. He knew. He swam alone through a cavern studded with barnacles and shining shells. He came to mighty crags and canyons where it seemed faces of wizened men and mighty warriors had been carved. A feeling of déjà vu came over him. *I have been here before*, Fin thought.

In bits it came back to him. Yes. This was the place. Somewhere near here was the rock with a face. On he swam, in and out between the great rock shapes. His thoughts turned to his grandmother Miranda. The last time he had seen her on the beach, a veil of white sat over her eyes and she had seemed afraid and weak. Miranda was queen of the selkies. She was strong and beautiful. She couldn't die. And Shuna? Would she be locked in that sunken ship for ever?

The memory of the weeping rock came back to him, and Fin fumbled to fit his goggles. They would keep the brown sludge from seeping into his eyes. He pulled them on and was plunged into night. They might stop his eyes from stinging, but his torch-lights, it seemed, couldn't penetrate through them. He couldn't see a thing.

Magnus Fin was close to the rock. He knew that. His nostrils told him so. A sickly metallic smell caught at his throat. He grasped his moon-stone with one hand and placed his other hand over his belly. *Stay alert*, that's what his instinct told him.

Sightless, he reached his hands out and felt through the thick water. Hearing a bang he drew back, afraid. Was that the beating of his heart? Or was it the same muffled thudding sound he had heard before?

He strained to hear. The sound grew louder. And louder.

Blindly he followed the awful noise, groping forward through the water, trying to imagine he had an eye at the tip of each finger. One moment the banging sounded like a whale trumpeting, the next like a messenger knocking at a castle door. Trails of plankton brushed his face. The dull battering went on and on.

Fin reached forward and the palms of his hands grazed against hard rock. His fingers landed in something jelly like. He winced. He felt a thin gap in the stone. More of

105

the oozing jelly smeared his fingers. Fin drew his hand back and clutched his moon-stone. This was it! He had finally arrived.

The banging stopped. An eerie silence hung around him. Where was the green eye? Staring at him through the crack in the rock? Fin couldn't tell. But the source of the selkies sickness lay behind this rock. Of that he was certain.

Chapter 22

Magnus Fin felt strength surge through him. Neptune had called on him. This was no time or place for weak knees and palpitating heartbeats.

He patted and groped either side of the crack in the rock. The gap was too thin to squeeze even an arm through. Yanking his hand free, he felt gunge stick to his skin. He kicked his feet and grasped around the rock, feeling for an entrance.

Fin shuddered as the banging sound resumed, like a hammer on his head. Remembering the splitting headache he suffered before, he had to move fast. This thick, sticky liquid was no ordinary seawater; it was toxic. He didn't need eyes to tell him that. Already a drowsy feeling had crept into him. He carefully opened the locket and took out a strand of Neptune's seaweed to protect him from the poison. Magnus Fin had felt around the huge rock from side to side and down to the seabed. There was no opening. Could he find a way in over the top? Fin kicked his feet and glided upwards. Twice he scraped his feet against the craggy stone. Then suddenly there was no more stone.

Groping forward Fin felt only water. He'd reached the top of the rock. Blindly he swam over it and prepared to dive down into what seemed to be a crater. He longed to whip off his goggles and scan the place with his torch-lights, but he remembered the stinging pain from last time. So he swam nervously downwards through the pitch-black. Down there somewhere, in amongst the gunge and the banging, was a creature with a green and wild staring eye.

The water pressure grew heavier, the stench stronger than ever. The banging had stopped. Through black thick nothingness Fin dived, like a lamb going into a lion's den. He kept going because the feeling in his belly told him to, and because his dad had told him to heed that feeling.

Fin didn't have eyes but he had ears. His ears heard a squeaking and a scraping. Fin stopped. The green-eyed poisoner, whatever it was, was close. Fin's heart jolted. A sound like a muffled scraping noise reverberated through the water, followed by a bang.

Panic swept through Magnus Fin. His blindness terrified him. Forget instinct, he was a sitting duck. The invisible green-eyed monster that brought the sickness to the selkies could bat him around like a tennis ball, or swallow him in one bite. If Magnus Fin was to save his grandmother and put an end to this sickness, he needed to see. Better stinging eyes than no eyes at all. He tore off the goggles, blinked furiously and flashed his torch-light eyes.

He scanned the water beneath him and gasped. Was this a sunken city? Were these fallen pillars, slumped walls and roofs? He seemed to be in some kind of huge round cavern. Below him were heaped rusting silver and white square and oblong shapes. Fin moved closer. The smell made him retch. What were they?

Something shifted between two of the white shapes. Fin froze. What was it? It looked liked a jumble of jerking seaweed. Fin's heart kicked in his chest. What kind of weird creature was this? Sticking out from the jumble of seaweed two arms or tentacles flapped about in the water. Was this a kind of octopus? Fin slipped back into the bearded shadows of the cavern wall.

The thing wriggled itself up from between two white shapes. Fin watched. A small creature with a head of long matted black hair lumbered over the white objects. The thing, Fin now saw in horror, had spindly legs or tentacles. They moved jerkily through the water, studded with limpets and barnacles. Seaweed and slime clung to the creature's body. Now the wild thing crawled onto one of the white blocks. Once on top, it hunched over and rocked something that looked like a door back and forth, back and forth. Water whooshed in and out, making waves. The banging echoed round the cavern. This was surely the poisoner.

Magnus Fin, hardly able to see anything now with all the churning and frothing, struggled to swim closer against the swell. The creature, who or whatever it was, ceased banging the door for a second, jerked its head up and trembled. Fin darted in between a dark swathe of seaweed.

Fin's eyes grew wide as plates. Slowly it dawned on him; this was no sunken city, no great undiscovered continent under the sea. He shook his head in amazement. A dump – for fridges, car batteries, freezers and storage tanks full of who knows what; that's what this was. He'd dropped down into a giant toxic rubbish bin! And snaking round the dump oozed thick, brown liquid.

Fin grasped his moon-stone, trying to find the courage to swim closer and steal a better look at the wild creature in the dump. He crept around the edge of the cavern, keeping close to the hanging fronds. Never had he seen anything like it, not even in a film. The awful monster was banging fridge doors as though it was conducting an underwater orchestra.

Perhaps the creature sensed the presence of something above, for suddenly it stopped banging and jerked its bushy head upwards. Its body twitched. If that was hair on its head it was matted with a tangle of weeds and fishing net. As the bush of hair parted Fin saw the same wild staring green eye that he had seen before. But there were two of them. They flitted here and there, restless and vacant, as though the creature behind those eyes was somewhere far away.

Fin held his breath and slunk back behind a thick clump of algae. He didn't dare move.

It didn't take long for the brown stinking sludge to seep into Fin's eyes. Quickly he rubbed them. They stung. They burned. He tried frantically to pull his goggles back on but it was too late. His torch-lights grew dim.

He let go his grasp of the seaweed and floundered in the water, sinking down level with the mound of tanks and fridges, thrashing his arms in wild circles.

The green-eyed creature was in no doubt now that it had company. It too thrashed its barnacled arms through the water. The dump was a churning froth.

In his panic Fin lashed out, kicked a storage tank and banged his leg. He slumped down beside it, exhausted.

The sea creature leapt over a fridge then hunched down to stare at his visitor.

Silence. The banging ceased. Fin groaned as the searing pain burned into his eyes. He tried to drag himself up. Everything was a blur but he knew the monster was close. He had to get away from this menace. As he struggled to stand up, his knees buckled under him. His eyesight was fading fast.

The wild creature tipped its head to one side, stared at the visitor, then with two filthy hands pushed Fin hard. Fin fell back with the sheer force, and the fear. He crashed against a fridge, lifting it up briefly before it came thundering back down, trapping Fin's leg underneath it.

The creature clambered back onto a huge freezer. Wildly now it banged the door, churning up the whole cavern.

Magnus Fin tried to free his leg but it was wedged in tight between the rocky ocean floor and the fallen fridge. In a daze he grasped the locket that hung beside the moon-stone around his neck. Struggling to open it, he managed to draw out one strand of Neptune's seaweed. Groping blindly, he brought the weed to his burning eyes and rubbed it over them. Instantly a cooling feeling brought relief. He was able to half-open his eyes. A dim light flickered from them. Like a sputtering candle the light grew. With his eyesight returned, Fin stared at the creature now swimming in circles above him.

The thing's matted hair, if you could call it hair, stuck out all around it. Half the ocean seemed to live in that hair. Limpets and seaweed clung to the creature's body. What was it? A four-legged hairy octopus? A turtle that had lost its shell?

Whatever it was, it suddenly jumped off the freezer and did a frantic doggy paddle in Fin's direction.

Fin gasped and tried again to free his leg but with no luck. Fin's head throbbed. His leg felt numb. The smell in this dump made him want to throw up.

But something held the green-eyed creature back. It seemed suddenly unsure of Magnus Fin. It kept its distance as it peered through the murky water.

Could the strange creature understand him? Fin wondered. Would it be able to read his thoughts? Fin tried to focus on his sick grandmother. He tried to pull his dissolving thoughts together. *Who are you? I am Magnus Fin. I am the grandson of Miranda, son of Ragnor. What are you?*

The creature stopped banging the freezer door. It jerked its head up, down and all around. Then, as though distressed, it yanked and pulled at its hair.

Fin grasped his moon-stone and tried again. *I am Magnus Fin. Miranda is my grandmother. Aquella is my cousin. What are you? Who are you?*

At the name Aquella the creature suddenly let go of its hair. The wild green eyes flickered, widened and seemed to burn. The creature grew still. Then they came: rusty, half-formed thoughts, as though this poor thing hadn't spoken to anyone for a very long time.

Aquella ... it stammered, *Aquella ...*

Chapter 23

Tarkin was glad the engine had cut out. He couldn't imagine now why he'd panicked. The engine had been noisy and dirty. It was more tranquil without it. He loved the slapping, low swishing sounds his oars made every time he dipped them into the sea. He loved the way the small boat glided through the water with every pull of the oars. And it was him, Tarkin, making the boat move, with his muscles, his back, his strength.

The only pity was the sweets were gone. He'd wolfed back the toffees, hardly tasting them. Nerves, that's what all that fast chewing earlier was about. He didn't feel nervous now. The moon glinted on the water and from far in the distance he could hear music coming from the village hall. Tarkin grinned, imagining his mother and Frank trying to do a Gay Gordons.

He rowed a bit and daydreamed a bit. He felt a river of sweat trickle down his spine. It might be November but Tarkin didn't feel cold. His life jacket was warm, plus three fleeces, not to mention the vigorous activity of rowing itself. He had heard about people on rowing machines at the gym. Now here he was, rowing for real, on the North Sea no less. His hands were slippery with sweat but he didn't dare let go of the oars. He'd seen films where people let go of oars and in seconds the oars were gone and the people goners. No, Tarkin was hanging on, and every now and then glancing over his shoulder. The coastline was closer; he was sure it was. All he had to do was keep the boat more or less near the rocks; not so near he'd smash against them, but near enough that Magnus Fin would be able to find him.

Where was Fin anyway? At least five, even ten minutes had passed. That could feel like days, weeks even, under the sea. Tarkin glanced over the edge of the boat but he could only see one person down there and that was his own silvery reflection. In his mind he repeated the words of his Native American chant, *Eagle feather, white and pure, guide him, guide him.*

Tarkin's mind started wandering to the mermaid he had seen back home in the Yukon, far west of where he was now. It was three years since that beautiful magical head had risen from the freezing lake. Tarkin remembered it like it was yesterday. It had only been a fleeting glimpse, but his dad had said he'd see her again. The water slapped against the hull of the boat. The gentle rocking motion soothed him. Maybe, if he thought really hard, he'd see her again. Tarkin's eyes shone. Magnus Fin had told him that's how magic creatures talk to each other. Fin called it "thought-speak". Tarkin concentrated hard on his thinking.

It's me, Tarkin, he began. And if it's possible for thoughts to be loud and slow, Tarkin's thoughts were. *I am in a boat, in Scotland. I am rowing. I'm rowing over the moonlit sea.*

Chapter 24

Magnus Fin's head was reeling. The effort of that strange stammered speaking seemed to have exhausted the creature and now it crouched down in a small fridge without a door. Its wild black hair and seaweed-covered body trembled. Had Fin heard right? He was still new at this kind of talking. Perhaps he had made a mistake. From what he'd heard, the creature somehow knew Aquella – or had heard of her.

Neptune's seaweed had worked wonders on Fin's eyes and now he could see perfectly, though what he saw horrified him. The creature looked more human than he had first thought: as the water swayed, the weeds sticking to the creature's body swayed too, revealing thin white arms and legs. Fin saw too how brown liquid oozed out from a hole in a metal tank and swirled around the creature's face. It seemed to drive it mad. It shook its head. It jerked its limbs. It tossed back its wild head and glared.

Magnus Fin panicked. He tried to free his leg but it wouldn't budge.

The thing stormed out of its fridge with a great thrashing, splashing and frothing. Like a lobster it scuttled over the dumped waste. In moments it was hunched down, crouching close to Fin's face.

Help! Fin yelped. *Don't hurt me! I am Aquella's cousin.*

But the creature seemed to have forgotten speech. It lifted its arms, stared at the back of its own hand, pulled off a limpet and sucked at its contents. Then it ripped off another and another.

Fin's stomach churned at the awful sucking sounds of the creature's pulled flesh. Fin bit his lip as he noticed the longest nails he had ever seen. They curled back on themselves like hooks. Glancing down at the thing's feet, Fin saw the same horned and horrible nails, long as sickle moons. Would he be the creature's next victim?

Fin considered lashing out. He might not have the use of his legs but he had his arms. But then he recalled how strong the creature was. That push had felled him like a sledgehammer. The green eyes seemed to be on fire now.

Try feelings, Fin thought, frantically: *Aquella is on the beach,* he struggled to say. *Aquella. She's my cousin.*

But this time the name seemed to upset the creature, which stamped the rubble-strewn ground. In a flash the wild thing picked up a car battery and hurled it towards Fin. The battery flew in slow motion through the water, just missing the top of the fridge that Fin was trapped under.

In his mind Magnus Fin screamed the name, *Aquella! Help me. Help!*

But Aquella didn't hear. Aquella was fast asleep.

This is it, thought Magnus Fin. No help was coming. The crab got him into this, now where was he? Fin had never felt so alone in his life. He stared miserably at the creature and waited for a terrifying punch, a kick or even a slash from those awful talons. The next battery was

116

bound to hit him. He groaned. He'd come so far and all for nothing. He'd found the cause of the sickness. It was the toxic waste that oozed from the storage tanks and batteries; he knew it was. That was what was killing the seals. And if the mad creature that lived in this dump didn't kill him, then the brown sludge would, or drive him as mad as the fiend that stood before him.

Get it over with, Fin thought. There was no fight left in him. He had failed. *Go on.* Magnus Fin closed his eyes. *Just do it!*

The creature whimpered. Fin opened one eyelid and stared. The thing in front of him lifted its seaweed-covered arms and took one swaying step then another towards him.

Fin's whole body went numb. His heart raced. He didn't believe it was possible to get more frightened – until what happened next.

The wild green-eyed creature bent forward, wrapped its slimy arms around Fin's neck and hugged him. It hugged Magnus Fin so tightly he could hardly breathe. He didn't dare move. He didn't dare upset it. The slimy seaweed from the thing's body pressed against Fin's face. The oil and muck smeared itself over his hair. Still the thing hugged him tight, so close Fin reeled at the stench that came from it. He felt its shoulders shake. Then Fin felt what could only be a briny tear run down its cheek.

Magnus Fin hadn't died. He could still feel his heart pounding. He struggled to form a thought. *I can help you,* he said, though he had no idea how.

The creature pulled back and looked at Magnus Fin. The tears seemed to have cleaned the staring eyes. They glittered.

117

But how could he do anything to help, trapped as he was. He couldn't even help himself. The pain in his leg was getting worse by the minute and his free foot now ached with pins and needles. The thick, poisoned water that swirled around him was affecting him; his head pounded and he was starting to feel drowsy.

Help! Fin called to Aquella, or to the crab, or to anyone or anything that might hear. *Help me! Neptune! Anyone – please help me!*

Chapter 25

I am rowing on the sea. I am rowing on the moonlit sea.

Maybe it was the white shining face of the moon. Maybe it was the rhythmic slap and slosh of water against the hull of the boat. Or maybe it was the mesmerising lull of the chanting going round and round in his head, but to look at Tarkin you'd think he was in some kind of trance. His pale blue eyes stared ahead. The silvery moonlight fell upon half of his face, plunging the other half in shadow. His long thin arms pulled the oars back and forth, cutting into the water and sluicing through it, though whether the boat moved or not was hard to tell.

I am rowing on the sea. I am rowing on the moonlit sea.

He forgot about toffee. He forgot even about his mermaid. He forgot about the lurking danger of sharks or killer whales. The image of his best friend Magnus Fin floated into his mind. *I am rowing on the moonlit sea.*

Deep down in the stinking fridge dump new words suddenly penetrated Fin's thumping headache: *I am rowing on the moonlit sea.*

Magnus Fin jolted up. He banged his head on the fridge behind him. Hope leapt into his throat.

It came again: *I am rowing on the moonlit sea.* Even in Magnus Fin's frantic state he could make out the slight rise and fall of an American accent. It could only be Tarkin!

Again Fin struggled to push the fridge off his foot but it refused to budge. The creature seemed to have retreated back to its fridge.

In agony Fin tried to focus his thoughts. *Help me, Tarkin! Help me! I'm down here. Help!*

To communicate this way you had to picture strongly the person you were trying to get through to. Fin imagined Tarkin's pale blue eyes, his gangly limbs, his long fair hair, his shark's tooth necklace, his wide smile.

Help me! I'm down here. I'm stuck under a fridge. Oh help!

Aquella slept soundly. She hadn't slept deeply like this since coming ashore five months earlier. She was back under the sea in the protective cosy pelt of her seal skin. She twisted, plunged and spun. She tumbled in the clear waters. She bared her sharp teeth and scooped up fresh salmon. She flicked her tail fins lazily back and forth. She turned swift somersaults with her brother. Or she hauled herself up onto a warm rock and basked in the sun. She was back with her selkie family, and in that deep sleep between moonlight and sand she had never felt happier.

In the distance the winkle picker walked along the beach path, swinging his empty pail. With the tide out and the moon full he could forage for hours. He had a torch which he shone now and then to check his way, though it was hardly needed on such a clear night. If he wondered about the small boat out at sea he didn't show it. Once down at the skerries he set to work, bending to pluck whelks from the rocks. As he worked, his song lilted over the stones:

Speed bonnie boat, like a bird on the wing
Onward the sailors cry,
Carry the lad that's born to be King
Over the sea to Skye.

Out at sea Tarkin's pale blue eyes grew wide as dinner plates. His face turned white. His mouth fell open though still no words dropped from his mute mouth. His head buzzed. A voice was in his head and it wasn't his! It had a Scottish accent: *Help me! I'm stuck under a fridge!*

Tarkin shook his head. He pinched himself but still the voice went on: *Help me!* Panicking he clutched the oars and peered over the side of the boat. He could see nothing. With trembling fingers he hauled in one oar and grabbed the torch. He flashed it over one side, then the other. There was nothing down there – nothing but water. His heart flapped like a trapped bird in a box. But still the anxious words came, jabbing into his head: *Help me. Tarkin. Help!*

It was the thought-speak. Somehow Magnus Fin's mind had broken through into Tarkin's. This was it! He was needed at long last. He hadn't stolen Frank's boat and risked his life just to practise rowing. Tarkin pinched himself awake. He snatched a deep breath to calm himself down. "This is it, Tark!" He slapped his legs, whipping up his sense of adventure and courage. "The moment you've been waiting for. Oh man. What a blast. Fin needs you. Don't blow it, Tark. Don't blow it!"

He heaved the oars into the boat and waited for instructions. Having another person's thoughts inside

121

your head was weird, scary even, but Tarkin tried hard to stay focused. *I'm here, buddy*, he thought, as loud and clear as he could. *I'm on the sea. Over and out!*

If Magnus Fin hadn't been prisoner under a fridge at the bottom of the sea he might have laughed at Tarkin's "over and out". A tiny smile broke over Fin's anxious face. The relief of making contact. Fin recalled seeing Tarkin's boat when he had jumped from the black rock. The boat had a winch. Maybe, just maybe, Tarkin could winch him up? But then what about the creature? He couldn't just leave him in this dump, could he?

You picking me up, buddy? It was Tarkin, somewhere up there on the sea, ready and waiting.

Lower the winch, Tark! Fin struggled to form his thoughts. Could Tarkin stay focused enough to receive them? He had to act fast. *Follow my thoughts, Tarkin. You're close by. I'll tell you when to stop. Then lower the winch. Please, Tarkin, you've got to get me out of here!*

The winch, Fin knew, had a hook on the end for winching up creels. If luck was on his side it might, just might, drop on target so Fin could grab it. Then it could lift him out. He'd have to push the fridge over with every last ounce of strength. He didn't want to break his leg. *Come on, Tarkin, hurry!*

Fin groaned. Something told him it would be easier to find a needle in a haystack than for Tarkin to drop the hook down through the water to exactly where Fin could reach up and grab it. But Tarkin was good at getting those funfair lobster-claw machines to pick up toys and sweets. It just might work. There was no plan B – it had to work.

On my way, buddy. Hang in there. Tarkin's on his way. Roger Dodger, over and out!

The excitement and thrill of being needed at last was stronger than any fear about being alone at night upon the sea. Tarkin dipped the oars back into the water and strained to receive his friend's guiding thoughts. *This way. Keep going. You're close.*

It was like one of those hot and cold games he and Fin played on the beach. Sometimes Fin's thoughts faded away until all Tarkin could hear was a faint whispering. Then back they came, in signal. *You're close now, Tark.* He kept rowing, occasionally glancing nervously over his shoulder as the craggy outline of the cliffs grew further and further away.

Tarkin was straining to catch Fin's thoughts so much that he could just make out a distant fiddle tune. He recognised it as a song they'd been learning at school, "Hey Johnnie Cope Are Ye Walking Yet?" He thought of the ceilidh, and his mother and Frank. "And are your drums a-beating yet?" And what would Frank say if he knew where Tarkin was now?

Fin? Magnus Fin? Hey – where are you? Drat! Blast! Tarkin cursed in his mind. In thinking about the ceilidh he'd lost contact with Magnus Fin.

Fin? Hey Fin? But it was no good. The signal was dead. Tarkin struggled to focus his mind, to push out thoughts of a red-faced and very disappointed step-father and a tear-stained mother.

Magnus Fin, he called in his thoughts, as loudly as he could. *Magnus Fin? Sorry, buddy, I lost you. Where are you?* But the lonely sea slapping the hull of the boat was the only reply. And Tarkin was now a very long way from land.

Chapter 26

The green-eyed creature of the dump slept in fitful snatches. Now, awake again, he went back to banging fridge doors. He banged so furiously he made underwater waves. Wedged miserably under his wretched prison Magnus Fin felt the force of water push him forwards then back. He could do nothing but flop back and forth like a rag doll. He felt sick and remembered the huge helpings of shepherd's pie he had eaten – when? It felt like days ago, though putting his hand over his belly he still felt full. The creature, now drumming madly, had managed to speak to him once. Even if it was only one word. Could it manage again? Tarkin, his rescuer, it seemed, had gone. Fin, with one hand on his belly and the other clutching his moonstone, called out in his selkie thoughts, *Fridge drummer? Please help me get out. My leg's really sore. Please?*

The banging stopped. Fin grabbed the opportunity and called again, *You are strong. You can push this fridge off me. Please. I won't hurt you. Please!*

Then he waited. He held his breath. He hardly dared lift his head.

The creature made a move. Fin felt a swell of water. Slowly he lifted his head. He heard scampering splashing sounds. He heard the grate of metal. He dared to peer out above his fridge. The green-eyed creature was clambering towards him over the freezers and storage tanks in a slow, lumbering fashion. It banged its slimy fist and shook its bush of hair.

Yes, Fin called again. *That's right – push the fridge. This one. Let me out! Please!*

The thing stretched out a seaweed-covered arm. The arm trembled. The curled horned nails scraped the side of the very fridge Magnus Fin was trapped under.

Yes! Fin went on, his whole body shaking, *Yes – go on – push it off me – go on …*

Crash! A booming thumped through the canyon. The waters heaved. The creature squealed and was flung, juddering backwards with the almighty force.

Hey! It's me, buddy! I heard you. Lost signal for a bit but we're back in contact. I'm bringing her down. Rescue party on its way! Roger Dodger, over and out!

The hook on the end of the winch plunged down through the water. The trembling creature crouched behind a rusting tank. It stared, terrified, as the black claw plummeted down through the water and clanged against the very fridge it had been ready to thrust aside.

The boom made by the winch-hook felt like a hammer on Magnus Fin's skull. His trapped leg throbbed, his heart pounded, but he had caught Tarkin's thoughts. Here was the rescue he'd given up hope for. And there, swinging and swirling through the murky waters, was the winch. Never had a hook looked so glorious. Magnus Fin struggled to form thought-speak. *Over to the right, Tark, move it over here, I can't reach it …*

Back and forth like a pendulum the hook swung above the piled-up junk. It lurched, catching strands of seaweed. It dangled enticingly above Fin's head.

He stretched up but his aching groping fingers found only water. Fin cried out as the hook swung off in the opposite direction.

A bit to the left now, Tark, just a bit. Again he tried to reach it. The tantalising hook hovered only inches from his stretching fingers. But it swung away again. Fin groaned. He couldn't believe it. So near and so far!

Tarkin. Back a bit. Come on, Tark. You can do it!

But maybe Tarkin wasn't sure of his left and right because now the hook splashed away.

Come on, Tark! Come on! Back the other way. Try again!

From behind the rusty tank, the creature watched. Three times the hook swung close to Magnus Fin. Three times he missed. The creature watched the hook jerk up, down, then fade off into the murky water. It was beginning to understand.

The creature sprang out from behind the storage tank and swam furiously through the polluted water. It took hold of the dangling rope and dragged it towards the prisoner.

Fin saw the hook. It dangled close – so close. He strained every muscle to reach towards it. He groaned. One more inch he stretched, and at long last his fingers clasped the rough wonderful touch of iron. Had he not been in such pain he would have cried out for joy.

Bringing you up, buddy!

Fin braced himself against the jerking motion. With his free leg he tried to kick the fridge off him, but it was a big industrial fridge. It didn't move. Fin tried to pull the hook down. Maybe the hook could topple the fridge? But there was no time. Tarkin was already reeling him up.

Wait, Tarkin. Not yet. Don't pull me up yet!

Frantically Fin tried again to kick the fridge over. But again the creature seemed to understand. It lunged forwards and with one almighty heave, sent Fin's fridge-prison tumbling, tumbling.

Magnus Fin was free! In the next instant he was floating up through the water. Below him the creature lifted its seaweed arms and stared. Its wild body and piercing eyes grew smaller and smaller as Fin, dangling from the hook, was lifted higher and higher.

Magnus Fin spun slowly up and up, until the dump was a dim blur and the fridge monster swallowed into the liquid darkness like a bad dream.

Tarkin, so excited he thought he would faint, wound up the winch rope. The closer the weight rose to the surface the lighter it became, but even so, it was hard work. He puffed. He panted. With aching arms he wound the handle. Gaping over the side he could see the dark shape of Magnus Fin's head under the water. Tarkin secured the winch handle, crying out as he did so, "I gotcha, buddy! Oh man, oh man! I gotcha!"

Chapter 27

Magnus Fin clung to the hook with both hands now. Seasickness had never bothered him but the jerking and jolting of the winch churned his stomach and turned his knees to jelly. His leg throbbed. Surely he was close to the surface by now? More thoughts slammed into Fin's mind. He needed to get to Miranda – fast. If he left the water now could he re-enter the magical world of the selkies? To find Miranda, to tell her he had found the source of the sickness, to bring her his baby tooth and Neptune's healing herbs, he had to remain in the selkie world. What now?

"I gotcha, buddy. Come on up. Wow! That was the most exciting thing I ever did!"

Fin had to think fast. He couldn't leave the water. And what about the poor creature down there? By this time Fin could see moonlight threading through the water. Any second now he'd break the surface. He couldn't get in the boat; he had to get to Miranda.

"Sorry, Fin, I ate all the candies."

Fin's head burst upwards. He shook his hair and a fountain of water splashed Tarkin in the face. But Fin kept his body underwater.

"Hey! Thanks," he shouted. "Wow! Well done, Tarkin. That was brilliant. It was really horrible being stuck down there. Tark?"

Tarkin was puffing, panting and rubbing his arms, but with a huge smile on his face. "No – ouch – no worries, man. It – it was – easy."

"Hey! Hey, Tarkin?" Fin called up from the water.

"Yeah?"

"Your voice! It's back."

In the effort and excitement Tarkin hadn't noticed. Now he yelled for joy and rocked the boat so much he almost fell overboard.

Fin, treading water and circling his arms called out, "Is there a net stuffed under the seat?"

"A what?"

"A net. Quick, Tark. It's not over yet. I need a net."

Tarkin bent down and shone his torch under the seat. "Wow! Cool," he shouted, "a net! And would you believe it? A can of diesel too!" He whistled as he dragged the net out. "Hey, Fin – no offence buddy – but you stink!"

"Thanks, Tarkin. Look, just throw me the net, will you? I can't leave the water. Not yet. I'm going to bring you something – I mean, someone." Fin wondered just how he was going to capture the wild "someone". The last thing he wanted to do was go back to that dump, but there was something in the way the mad creature had helped him, and hugged him, that meant he couldn't just leave it down there.

"Listen! When I bring it, I mean him, up, I'll wrap him in a net, OK? Then you have to go, Tark, go like the wind to the beach by the cave. Take him to Aquella. I have to find Miranda."

"OK, I'm ready. Like, who have you found down there? Is he a selkie?"

"I'm not sure, Tarkin, just keep him in the net and take him to Aquella." Fin hoped Aquella would be able to cope with the creature. Aquella could cope with most things and it seemed to know her. Precious seconds were ticking by. Fin wrapped his hand over his moonstone. "Have you got an anchor in there, Tark?"

"You think I got a travelling shop here, buddy?" Tarkin laughed as he looked around. It was obvious he didn't know if there was an anchor or not. He shone his torch and sure enough, there it was under the bench, a small rusty thing on the end of a coiled rope.

"Great! OK, Tark. Drop it over the side. I don't want to lose you." And with the net bunched under one arm, Magnus Fin lowered himself beneath the water.

"Bye, buddy. Good luck," Tarkin shouted, but Fin didn't hear him.

Fin flipped upside down and kicked back his heels for all he was worth. Down through the water he swam, the very way he'd come just moments before, dangling on the end of a hook. He shone his torch-light eyes through the murky sea. Easily this time he found the round rocky crater where the dumped fridges lay, stacked higgledy-piggledy like plastic monsters.

Everything was silent in the dump. The brown and stinking water, like a stagnant pond, barely moved. The creature was hiding somewhere. Magnus Fin scanned the crater, searching for bubbles that would give away its whereabouts. But all was still, like a watery graveyard. Slowly Fin paddled, gently flipping his webbed feet. Under his elbow he clutched the net.

As he swam the brown liquid wove around his body,

snaking up his nostrils and sidling into his ears. Magnus Fin struggled not to be sick. The poison in the canyon dimmed his thoughts and hurt his head. He had to act fast. He couldn't use another strand of seaweed, could he? He wanted to keep it for Miranda. The thought of his ailing grandmother gripped him with a sense of urgency. He had no time to lose. He stretched his arms through the water and felt slime coat the back of his hands. Frantically he scanned the dump. Where *was* the wild creature?

The deeper Fin dropped into the canyon the thicker the pollution. His head throbbed. His eyelids shut. There was nothing else for it – he would have to use another strand of Neptune's seaweed. *You'll have my baby tooth, Miranda,* he thought as he fumbled to unclasp his locket. If he didn't work fast he'd be as mad as the thing he had come to rescue. Quickly he drew out one more strand. This time he ate it. Instantly the drowsiness and stinging fled. Neptune's seaweed was powerful.

Swiftly now he swept his torch-light eyes over the tops of the fridges, freezers and tanks. The only way to capture the creature would be to catch it unawares. Just then Magnus Fin heard a tiny grunt. He drew back among seaweed and listened. The grunt changed to a whimper. Fin peered out from between two rubbery fronds and there it was just below him, crouched behind a huge fridge pulling limpets from its arm, making grunting, crunching, smacking noises as it ate. He had to hurry. From what he had seen these limpets gave it strength.

Fin swam down. The creature, so absorbed in its dinner, wasn't aware of the boy in a wetsuit hovering above it. *Right, Fin, three – two – one – go!* He kicked his feet. He plunged down. He loosened the net and dropped it over the creature, over its hair, over its seaweed-strewn body. It screamed in astonishment. It kicked and thrashed out, tangling itself in the net. The water frothed and churned. In a flash Fin yanked at the rope, which tightened the net in an instant, trapping the terrified creature inside.

Magnus Fin kicked his heels and heaved himself upwards, dragging the net and its squirming, screaming prisoner. For every two strokes up, the creature dragged him one stroke back. Just when Fin thought his whole body would break in two with the effort, he spied the white line of the anchor rope. He lunged out and grasped it. With one hand tugging the net and the other hand and two webbed feet clinging on to the anchor rope, Magnus Fin made his slow, aching way to the surface.

Up on the boat, because of all the pulling on the anchor rope, Tarkin was being flung this way and that. Groaning, he clung to the sides of the boat.

"Steady, Fin," Tarkin cried out, feeling sick and scared. "I can't swim remember. Whoa! Steady!"

Chapter 28

Magnus Fin saw splinters of moonlight crash down through the sea. He had to be close to the surface. Relief surged through him. With one last mighty effort he heaved his load upwards and his head burst out of the water. Sheets of seawater streamed down his face.

Gasping, he called out, "I've got it. I'll attach the net to the winch. When you get to the beach drag the net onto the sand. Then call for Aquella. She should be there in Ragnor's cave. It can't get out of the net, don't worry."

Tarkin had turned green. He groaned and clasped his hand over his mouth. Bending over the side of the boat, he retched and spewed up every toffee he had eaten.

Fin didn't have time for sympathy. "Hurry up, Tarkin. Turn on the engine. Pull up the anchor. Come on, Tark. I really need you to help." Fin wound the rope round the winch hook, noticing that the creature in the net had gone limp.

Tarkin staggered the few steps to the end of the boat. "Never again, Fin," he moaned. "I'm never getting on a boat again. Ever!" But even in his misery he managed to reach over and pull up the anchor. Then he was sick again.

"And you called *me* smelly?" Fin said. "You'll feel better afterwards, honest."

"I'll never feel better," Tarkin groaned, "not ever."

"Look, Tarkin, sorry to leave you like this. Take the net to the beach. Quick! I've got to go. Later, when Miranda's better, we'll have to get this dump cleaned up. I have to leave now, Tark, but selkie time moves fast. I might be back before you. Soon as I'm home I'll call 999. If you're back before me, you call. Tell them there's a dump in the sea. Leave a buoy so we know where it is."

Fin fumbled with the locket and drew out the last strand of seaweed. "When you get to the beach give this to Aquella. It's for the thing in the net."

"The what?" Tarkin groaned.

"The thing. Now go!" Fin dipped his head under the water, jack-knifed his body to face downwards and kicked back his heels. He had no time to lose. As he swam he clasped his locket shut. Only his baby tooth remained inside it. Grasping his moon-stone Fin felt its strength pour into him.

He dived deeper then glanced to the left. Was his grandmother this way? He flashed his torch-lights down a long rocky passageway to the right. Or was she this way?

Nice job.

Fin swung round. There in front of him was the crab, clinging to a long frond of seaweed and swaying back and forth through the water like a child on a swing.

You had me worried for a moment – but not really worried.

You left me trapped under that horrible fridge. And what about that poison? Not really worried? I nearly died!

But you didn't. And hey! Great pal you've got up there. Cheer up, M F. Don't let a few little bumps and scares get you down.

Magnus Fin shook his head in disbelief. *Little scares? I was petrified. And little bumps? I've got bruises all over me.*

They'll heal … and remember – you're brave. But hey! Some show you put on! Nice thinking with that net. I loved the way you just dropped it right over the poor thing.

There was something charming about the crab. Fin's anger evaporated. He couldn't help but like him.

Anyway, the crab continued, *now you know what's causing the sickness, you and your pals can clear this dump. Right then, let's get out of here.* And with that the crab jumped from his seaweed swing and paddled at high speed down the long rocky passageway. Fin followed, and soon the rock, rubble and underwater canyons were far behind them.

OK. Go for it, M F. Go to Miranda. She's at Sule Skerrie. Turn your nose to the west and plough down the seas.

Magnus Fin turned his nose to the west and kicked back the ocean. He looked over his shoulder to wave goodbye to the crab, but when he glanced back, true to form, the crab had gone. Fin swam as fast as he was able.

Miranda! he called in his thoughts, *Miranda!*

And on the very edge of hearing, the faintest glimmer of a reply sounded through the waves: *Magnus Fin …*

Chapter 29

The winkle picker stood up to stretch his back. His pail was filling fast. Full moon was always a good night for the periwinkles. "*Baffled our foes stand by the shore,*" he sang, rubbing his sore back as he did so, "*follow ... they ... will ...*"

He rubbed his eyes. Then he rubbed them again. He blinked. His long-range eyesight was forever playing tricks on him, "*... not ... da ...*" The song died on his lips. Either he was moon-mad, or that was a boy in a boat hurtling through the sea with a full net in its wake!

Once Tarkin had filled the tank with diesel and turned the throttle, there was no stopping him. He zoomed across the sea. Behind him the net bounced and slapped.

"Aquella!" Tarkin shouted at the top of his lungs when the dim outline of the cliffs, cave and beach came into view. "Where are you?"

He slowed down. The net bobbed gently. Tarkin scanned the beach. Fin had said Aquella would be on the beach, the beach by the cave. He called again, "Aquella!" So where was she? An oystercatcher, disturbed from its sleep, piped loudly.

By this time Tarkin had reached the shallow waters. The bottom of the boat scraped and juddered against the pebbles. The night before, Frank had berthed the boat in the small harbour. Tarkin had watched carefully as Frank had cut the engine, flipped a buoy over the side then thrown a rope around a bollard. But this beach was hardly a harbour and right now the boat was keeling on to its side. Tarkin panicked. What was he supposed to do now? He remembered seeing a film where the pirate tugged a raft ashore and hauled it up the beach.

"Here goes!" Tarkin shouted and jumped over the side. "Oh man! It's freezing!" He waded through the ice-cold water towards the beach, pulling the short rope that was attached to the lip of the boat. It was heavy. Very heavy. The water wanted to drag the boat back, and the squirming net made it even worse. Tarkin's feet slipped and scuffed on the slimy pebbles.

"Heave-ho!" he shouted, dragging his cargo inch by inch up onto the beach. "Here we go!" He stumbled on a boulder. The rope fell from his grip. With a thud Tarkin landed on his back. "Agh! Help!" he yelled. "Ouch! Agh! Somebody help!"

That's what finally woke Aquella. She rose from her seaweed pillow and looked around. Where was she? Where were the other selkies and the sparkling water? She rubbed her eyes then sat bolt upright. She was on the flat rocks by the beach. She had fallen asleep. And if she wasn't mistaken, that was Tarkin lying groaning on the sand!

Aquella jumped to her feet. A bolt of panic shot through her, seeing how far the moon had travelled. Had she been asleep all that time?

Magnus Fin, she called in her thoughts, *I'm sorry! I am so sorry. I fell asleep. Are you all right? Fin – where are you?*

Frantically she ran across the beach towards Tarkin. He was rolling from side to side, yelping like an injured dog and all the while the boat was slipping back into the sea.

"Tarkin!" she cried. "What's wrong?"

"Get it!" he shouted. "Quick, Aquella, just get the boat! And that net! There's something – ouch – in it for you!"

She swung round to see the boat glide back into the water. "But," she stammered, "but I ... the ..."

Already the salt water was dangerously close to her feet. Had Tarkin forgotten? The waves ran up and curled just inches from where Tarkin lay groaning on the beach, holding his shoulder and rubbing his elbow. In that moment they both heard the sound of footsteps crashing over pebbles behind them. In the moonlight a figure darted past them and ran into the sea. The winkle picker dragged the boat and its trailing net up the beach, pebbles and shells crunching under the weight.

Tarkin and Aquella, jaws gaping, could do nothing but stare.

When the man had pulled the boat past the wavy line of seaweed that marked the tideline he sighed loudly and let the rope go. The boat keeled onto its side and the bundle in the net lay motionless behind it. The man, hands on his hips now, was wheezing loudly with the effort. Slowly he turned to face the two children.

"Look after him," he said, gazing first at Aquella then at the net. "Rest," he muttered, "aye – that's what he needs." Then he hurried away up the beach. In a moment he was swallowed up by the shadows of the cliffs.

138

Tarkin and Aquella stared at each other. They shot nervous glances up towards the cliffs where the man had vanished.

"Are you all right?" Aquella was the first to break the silence.

Tarkin nodded. He bit his lip and lifted himself up to a sitting position. "Weird," he whispered. "Totally weird."

"It's that man who picks winkles," Aquella whispered back. "I think he's a friend of Ragnor. But what did he mean – look after him? Look after who?"

"Don't ask me. That guy is seriously weird. He's got something to do with killing the seals. Ouch. My back's real sore."

"But you've got your voice back! How come, Tarkin? What did you do?"

Tarkin looked up at Aquella strangely. "Do?" Then he looked over at the net. It lay unmoving on the sand. "I winched Magnus Fin out of the sea, then I dragged that thing all the way back here. Fin said you'd know what to do with it …"

Aquella stared at the net. Then she ran, stumbling over the beach towards it.

"Fin said he'd be back!" Tarkin shouted. "And we have to call the police – tell them about the dump. I left a buoy to mark the spot …"

But by this time Aquella had already reached the net. She wrenched the tight cord apart and gasped. A pile of stinking seaweed oozed out. She coughed, clutched her hand over her mouth and staggered backwards. The stink was overpowering. Even for a selkie like Aquella, who loved the pungent smell of the sea, this reek caught at the back of her throat. What was a pile of rotten seaweed doing stuffed in a net?

The bundle didn't move. She took a half-step towards it, keeping both hands pressed over her nose and mouth. She took another half-step, then another, then willed herself to peer into the putrid tangles.

At that moment, from the midst of seaweed, a thin white arm, smeared with gunge and pitted with barnacles, rose into the air.

Aquella screamed, reeled backwards and fell over a stone. But not once did she take her eyes off the strange arm that had now flopped over the side of the net.

From the net came a low whimpering noise. The arm had a hand. The hand had long curled nails and the nails were clawing at the net. Still Aquella stared as another arm rose up. The seaweed shook and shuddered. Inch by terrible inch, the seaweed rose upwards. The scarred arms pushed the net down.

Aquella had never been so terrified in her life but no matter how awful the sight she couldn't pull her eyes away. Her heart leapt into her mouth as she watched the wild and stinking mass of seaweed shake from side to side. As it shook, a hundred tiny creatures flew from the fronds and matted mess.

Then the seaweed fell to the sides to reveal a face. It had green staring eyes, a small round nose and a wide mouth. The face shone ghostly pale in the moonlight. The creature rose unsteadily to its feet and clambered out of the net. Standing trembling on the sand it stared at Aquella, and from out of those green eyes large tears rolled down its face.

"Ronan?" Aquella gasped, staggering to her feet.

140

"Ronan?" She ran across the beach, crying, laughing, yelping, no longer caring about the terrible smell. "Oh Ronan!" she cried, and flung her arms about the seaweed and oil-stained neck of her brother Ronan.

Chapter 30

It was a long, long way to Sule Skerrie.

As Magnus Fin swam he tried not to dwell on just how far it was. Time, in the selkie world, moved to a different rhythm. Maybe, Fin hoped, kicking his webbed feet back and forth like flippers, space did too? On he swam, shining his torch-lights ahead of him. They would alert him to any dangers. Killer whales hunted by night. And sharks were hungry anytime. Fin tried hard to banish killer whales and sharks from his mind. Even that ugly gang of ragged fish haunted his thoughts.

Fin swam through that dark clamouring silence, brushing aside trails of stringy seaweed that swept slowly to and fro, to and fro. His leg that had been trapped still throbbed but he pushed himself on. Under him an eel coiled then uncoiled its long tail, flicking up shells and small fish that floated off in slow watery motion. A large shoal of small silver fish surrounded Fin, then, as one, they were off, darting like arrows into the dark.

When fear gripped hold of him he thought of Miranda and held his precious moon-stone tight. Bravely Magnus Fin swam north. Feeling exhaustion slow him down he rounded Duncansby Head and continued into the Pentland Firth. Here was where the North Sea met the turbulent waters of the Atlantic Ocean. The current swirled and rushed. Magnus Fin swam into the racing swell but felt the surge of the sea push him back. Now his arms were aching. With every stroke they grew heavier. Even an Olympic swimmer would struggle against the tidal pull here. His heart pounded in his chest. He had pushed his body to the limit. And it was still a long way to Sule Skerrie.

Magnus Fin battled on, stretching his arms forward, kicking his webbed feet. But his strength was spent. Each stroke was agony. And each stroke was slower than the one before. He swallowed disappointment like a bitter pill inside him.

After all this, he would have to give up. *I'm sorry,* he called, dropping his arms by his side. His shoulders slumped. His legs stopped kicking. *I'm sorry, Miranda.* He couldn't go on.

I'm sorry. I fell asleep. Fin? Are you all right?

Fin let the tide drag him back. To take on the surge of the Atlantic Ocean was too much. But what was that?

Fin? Fin? Are you all right?

It was Aquella! She was back. But in Fin's mind it was already too late. The currents buffeted and pulled him. Drifting backwards he was powerless to resist. He would have to tell Aquella it was over. *I can't do it, Aquella. I can't reach Miranda. I just can't.*

Her thoughts darted back, strong and positive. *Listen, Fin. To make it to Sule Skerrie in time you'll have to summon every ounce of bravery you have. You have to let the change happen, Magnus Fin. Trust the change.*

The what?

The change, Fin. Only as a seal will you make it now to

143

Miranda. You have to relax. Picture the strong sleek body of a seal. Imagine it so hard you'll make it real. You are Sliochan Nan Ron, *remember. You're one of us.*

Help me, Aquella!

I am helping you.

Do I want to be a seal? thought Magnus Fin. But he already knew the answer: to survive and to save his grandmother, he *had* to become a seal.

He did as Aquella told him. He focused all his thoughts on changing into a seal. He pictured the beautiful strong sleek bodies of his selkie friends, their whiskered noses, glistening eyes and powerful flippers ...

And that's when it happened.

It started with his feet. He thought he had brushed against moss. He felt the webs between his toes thicken. Then his legs drew together, as though something was sucking him in then zipping him up. His feet fanned out and stiffened.

Huge strength poured into him. His whole body rounded and filled with it. His flesh expanded. His ribs pushed outwards. Magnus Fin cried out as an exhilarating power and joy pounded through him.

His arms contracted. He felt them suck in to merge with his strong round body. His hands grew bigger as though his own flesh was bursting from its skin to ripen into another stronger skin. These new hands drew in to his body. His fingers tapered. He felt a sleek warm fur cover him. A thick layer of protection and warmth enclosed him.

Then his face softened and his skin thickened. His neck dissolved. Bristles sprouted. His nose pushed forward and quivered as the tang of the ocean rushed into him. His teeth sharpened. A trembling keenness shot through him.

He was a seal, strong and powerful.

Now Magnus Fin could take on the might of the Atlantic Ocean.

Chapter 31

Through the rip-tides and currents of the Pentland Firth he ploughed, surging out towards the Orkney Islands. Magnus Fin felt the keenness of his hearing and the sharpness of his nostrils. His long soft whiskers brushed sea grass aside. His tails fins flicked through the water, turning him easily this way and that. As last he knew the freedom and strength of the seal. He heeded the compass of his marine instinct and plunged west towards the wild and rugged headland of Cape Wrath.

Swimming was a joy. His strength felt boundless. He twisted, he turned. Like a bolt through the blue he plunged westward. He cleaved through the racing currents, rounded Cape Wrath then turned north towards Sule Skerrie. On he swam, the only seal in the ocean wearing a moon-stone and a silver locket, which were now tight around his thick seal neck.

Magnus Fin allowed the soft folds of his nostrils to open as he lifted his seal head out of the water. Everything had been worth it for this. He breathed loudly, swivelling his head to the right and left. The moon splashed over the dark sea and threw a clear path ahead. Fin pushed air through his nostrils, thinking how many times, as a boy, he had stood on the rocks and watched seals lift their heads from the water; how many times he had heard their noisy blowing breath, their haunting howling bark.

Peering down the moon path he tried to spot the island of Sule Skerrie. It was the home of the selkies. The place his father was born. The place selkies went for sanctuary, and when it was time, the place they went to die. He raised his head higher. Was it that far dent on the horizon? He plunged on.

Magnus Fin could swim with the speed and strength of a seal. He had the warm powerful body of a seal. Could he, he wondered, sing with the haunting voice of a seal? Why not? Everything and anything seemed possible tonight. So, lifting his head, he blew through his lips. To his astonishment, a long deep note, like a bagpipe drone, sounded from him and carried through the night air. On and on it echoed.

After his song faded into the silence another note sounded, like an answer from the west, from that far dint on the horizon.

He plunged back into the deep sea and followed that note. Migrating shoals of herring parted as he swam. Wild Atlantic salmon darted away from him. Shrimps and blue lobsters scuttled over the ribbed seabed far beneath him. Northwest Magnus Fin travelled, and always with Miranda in his thoughts.

Fin sensed he was close. Once more the seal's song, muffled and haunting, reached him. Again Magnus Fin broke the surface of the water. In the air the song grew louder – and there in the distance was the island of Sule Skerrie.

Soon seals swam out to greet him. Their cries and yelps broke on the wind. Above them kittiwakes and gannets screamed. From this group of curious seals, one approached: a large grey seal with mournful yellow eyes. She swam up to Magnus Fin then guided him in to the island.

Welcome, son of Ragnor, welcome to Sule Skerrie, she said. Together they dived into the waves that dipped and broke around the island. Fin, although grateful to be welcomed by the seals, wanted only to see his grandmother, quickly, before it was too late.

He looked pleadingly at his guide. *Miranda, you know, is my grandmother. I have come all this way. Can I see her?*

The grey seal seemed to hesitate, tipping her head to the side. Then slowly, gravely she nodded. The sea lapped about them. *Come then*, she said, *this way.*

Chapter 32

Gliding silently the seal guided Magnus Fin to a quiet part of the small island, away from the throng of seals. Fin felt a sadness engulf him. This grey seal had told him nothing about Miranda. Was he too late?

What about the sickness? Fin asked his guide. *These seals I saw look healthy.*

Aye, Fin. She slowed down now and looked at him. *Miranda took the sickness on to herself, and brought us here, away from the coast. Away from the bay close to where you live, Magnus Fin. Away from the sickness.*

And Miranda? My grandmother, how is she?

You won't know her, Fin. She went too close too often to the sickness trying to gather us up. Each time she grew weaker. In the end she couldn't swim. Then one seal found the fallen ship, another of the human's sunken things. Selkies still in the bay would be kept safe in the upturned ship. The sickness couldn't get into it. Too many selkies were suffering. So many have died.

The seal swam to a jutting rock and slowed down. *Miranda is in that cave. You know our deep-sea caverns, Fin. At the end we selkies choose a place where land and sea meet. Come. Haul up onto the flat stones and use your flippers to rock over.*

Magnus Fin said nothing. He followed his guide as

she slithered from the smooth water up onto the hard flat stone. They rocked back and forth over the stones, awkwardly it seemed to Fin. He made slow progress trying to bounce up and down on his belly. Running with two legs would have been much easier, but Fin didn't have two legs. Suddenly on the land he missed them.

Come on, Magnus Fin. Use the muscle of your whole body. Didn't you ever push yourself along on your belly as a baby? The seal waited for him, shaking her old grey head at the poor job Fin was making of slithering.

Well, if Fin ever had slithered along on his belly as a baby he certainly couldn't remember it. Finally, after much rocking and noisy breathing, Fin arrived at the mouth of the cave.

She's inside, on a bed of sponge and kelp. Come quietly now and do nothing to upset her.

They bounced and rocked into the cave. Inside it was pitch-black with no glimmer of moonlight. *Your eyes will get used to the light,* the grey seal whispered in her thoughts. *You will see her in a moment. Don't be shocked, son of Ragnor.*

Fin was glad for the darkness. What met his ears was terrible. Each laboured breath coming from inside the cave sounded full of torment. Horrified, Fin could only imagine what his poor grandmother now looked like. It was as though, in every slow rattled breath, Fin heard the scrape and clank of the dumped tanks, fridges, freezers and batteries. In her every wheezing gasp he imagined the polluted water filling his beloved grandmother's lungs.

After a few moments, Fin's eyes adjusted to the light

and the cave was no longer a black emptiness. In the seeping grey light Magnus Fin could make out the shrunken figure of his grandmother. But she, Fin saw with shock, could not see him, or anything. Her eyes were white unseeing discs. Her mouth hung open and her teeth were crumbling. It was then Fin became aware of the terrible smell. A stench clung to the back of his throat.

In his shock he had forgotten the medicine he carried. He bit open the locket and sucked up the baby tooth. The locket broke and fell onto the floor of the cave. Fin knew what he had to do: transfer the tiny tooth he carried in his own mouth into the mouth of his grandmother, and he had to do it quickly.

He slithered a few inches forward.

Don't distress her, Fin. Stay back.

But Fin kept going. This was what he came for. All these M Fs on the rocks were for this. Tarkin stealing the boat was for this. His father telling him to heed his instinct was for this. Getting locked in the sunken ship, then trapped under the fridge and almost losing his sight in the dump – even finding the green-eyed creature – everything was for this.

Fin put his flipper on his belly. *Go on*, it shouted, *go on!* Even though Miranda was distressed at the nearness of another seal, even though she was now whimpering in fear and shaking, Fin knew he had to go right up to her.

The grey seal cried out behind him, *Magnus Fin, you are upsetting her. She has enough to bear. Stop in the name of Neptune – I command you to stop!*

Magnus Fin drew level with his grandmother's nose. This too was in the name of Neptune. Hadn't the great

151

Neptune himself called on Magnus Fin?

In a flash, he nuzzled his own soft mouth inside Miranda's, then parted his lips to allow the baby tooth to roll into her mouth. Quickly he drew back his face, lifted his flippers and with them closed her mouth.

The grey seal gasped. She rocked forward to stop him, honking loudly in her distress. *You're killing her. Stop it!*

She tried to push Fin away. Though old, she was strong. With her head she pushed at Fin's head. *Leave her!* her thoughts cried out. *It was a mistake to bring you here. Have you gone mad?* She hit him hard, thumping his head, forcing him to loosen his grip on Miranda's mouth.

She reared up and was about to roll down on top of Fin when suddenly Miranda moved. The grey seal drew back in shock. She stared in disbelief as Miranda slowly, purposefully, worked her crumbling jaws and swallowed her grandson's medicine.

The grey seal stared, a tear rolling down her face. Her honks of distress changed to whimpers of disbelief. *I'm sorry, Magnus Fin,* she said, not able to take her eyes away from Miranda who was gently nodding her head. *Forgive me.*

Magnus Fin slumped back against the wall of the cave. The old grey nurse seal rocked over to him and now nuzzled the throbbing places which moments earlier she had fiercely whacked.

Miranda's laboured breathing grew quieter. The rattle softened. Over and over the grey seal whispered her apologies to Magnus Fin, but though Fin tried to focus his mind, the thought-speech seemed suddenly closed to

152

him. So he lifted his painful flipper and gently stroked the nurse seal's sleek head. Of course he forgave her; even though his head throbbed and his flipper ached he understood she had been trying to protect Miranda.

Now they both watched in the shadow-grey light as Miranda lifted her head from its pillow of sponge. Her nostrils quivered as she sniffed the air. Fin thought of his last baby tooth, now crunched down and hopefully working its magic inside her. Miranda stretched her long silvery neck. Then she spread her flippers wide on the mattress of seaweed and raised herself up. She moved forward an inch, then two.

Spellbound, Magnus Fin and the grey seal watched from the dark shadows of the cave. They didn't dare move, lest whatever was happening might suddenly stop. They listened as Miranda exhaled loudly. The putrid smell that rushed from her nostrils was the smell of the dump. The rush of breath and foul smell threatened to overpower the two watching seals. Again and again Miranda exhaled, as though expelling all the poison she had carried.

Once more Miranda lifted her head, easier this time, and opening her mouth she cried out. Her cry, like a victory trumpet, lifted into the night air and travelled across the ocean.

All the seals playing in the moonlit waters around Sule Skerrie heard it.

Shuna and the other seals in the quarantine of the sunken ship, far away in the North Sea, heard it.

Aquella and Ronan on the beach by the cave heard it.

Ragnor, who had stepped outside for a lungful of fresh air, heard it.

Even the winkle picker, making a fire in the cave by the beach heard it.

All those with ears to hear heard the news: Miranda, the bright one of the sea, was well again.

Chapter 33

For a long while Aquella hugged her brother. The brown gunge stuck to her. The barnacles dug into her. The rotten seaweed almost smothered her. But none of that mattered. She had found her brother and he needed her like never before. That was all that mattered. She felt him trembling as she pressed him close. She heard him struggle to find words: "I – it – cold – so – so …"

"Hush," she whispered, finding his ear behind the wild bush of hair, "hush Ronan. If you're cold I'll make a big fire. Look! You have come to the beach by Ragnor's cave."

Ronan was now shaking like a leaf. Aquella found his hand. She gasped when the long curled nails dug into her soft palm. She tried to guide her brother up the beach towards the cave. His legs buckled under him. He stumbled and fell, like someone who hasn't walked for a very long time. She bent down, scooped him into her arms and carried him to the cave, stumbling under his weight.

Tarkin saw none of this. As soon as he realised that something alive was clambering out of the net he clasped his hands over his eyes. He'd learnt his lesson. He wouldn't go spying and prying into the selkie world again. He had his voice back, and he wanted to keep it.

But the winkle picker, leaning against the mouth of the cave, saw it. He withdrew into the cave and struck a match, setting light to the spire of driftwood he had gathered. In minutes the cave was warm, and fiery shadows leapt up the rocky walls. The winkle picker placed a spar of wood onto the fire then, with not a sound, he left the cave, picked up his pail and hurried back down to the skerries to resume his night's work.

"We're nearly there, Ronan," Aquella gasped. Not only his weight, which was due more to the wet seaweed and gunge sticking to him than Ronan himself, but the putrid stench made her stagger. "Soon, soon, Ronan, you'll be all right. I'll clean you up. I'll make a fire and ..." Aquella sniffed. Another smell wove around her. The good smell of wood smoke. She stared over her brother's head. A thin coil of smoke drifted from the mouth of the cave. "Look, Ronan!" she cried out. "Someone's made a fire for you. Look!"

Aquella staggered into the cave. "We're here. Lie down. Here, Ronan." She lowered him onto the sandy floor of the cave. His trembling had stopped. He lay motionless, staring up at her with his piercing green eyes. In the glow of the fire Aquella could see now how ill, dirty and ravaged her brother really was. "It's all right, Ronan. Everything is going to be all right."

She set to work, plucking barnacles from his arms and gently pulling off strands of rotten seaweed. With razor shells she cut his horned nails. Through it all she soothed him with the old songs their mother had once sung to them.

Yon do, yon da, yon do, ro don do
Yon do, yon da, yon do, ro don do ...

When Tarkin did open his eyes, Aquella and the strange creature had gone. Tarkin smelt the wood smoke. Glancing up, he saw smoke drift from the cave. He guessed Aquella was there dealing with whatever had been in the net. That was selkie business and Tarkin didn't want to butt in. Tarkin plunged a hand in his pocket hoping to find a toffee. He found instead a long strand of seaweed. Fin had given him this to give to Aquella. Tarkin groaned. He had forgotten all about it. He didn't want to go into the cave, but Fin had begged him to deliver this.

Unsteadily Tarkin rose to his feet. Despite his fall no bones appeared to be broken. Covering his eyes he stumbled towards the cave. "Aquella!" he shouted when he was close enough to hear her singing. "I've got something for you. Magnus Fin says it's for the thing in the net."

In seconds Aquella was by his side, but still Tarkin kept his eyes covered. He held the seaweed in the palm of his outstretched hand and felt her snatch it from him.

"I can't believe it!" She clutched at the strand of seaweed and deeply breathed it in. "This is medicine from Neptune. Oh thank you, thank you. Oh – and Tarkin? It's not a thing – it's my brother!" Then she was gone.

Tarkin ran down the beach. Some things were too weird even for him. If that thing in the net was Aquella's brother, he would definitely leave them to it.

157

He stared out over the moonlit sea. Where was Magnus Fin? Tarkin struggled to focus his thoughts. *Fin! Hey – Magnus Fin!* But his thinking could push open no magic door. Not this time. He was an ordinary boy again. He shivered.

A wave broke and cold water curled round his feet. Tarkin gasped and looked down. His trainers were soaked. Then he looked over his shoulder to where Frank's boat lay on its side. A thump of guilt punched him in the stomach. What time was it? Had Rena, the neighbour, gone to check on him? Had Frank discovered his boat was missing? Tarkin felt himself drowning under a flood of nagging doubts.

Magnus Fin had his selkie magic. He would manage without Tarkin's help. And Aquella was singing softly to some weird stinking thing. She didn't need his help. "Oh jeepers creepers," he gulped, staring out across the rippling water to the harbour. He had to haul the boat back into the water. He had to cross the bay and steer the boat into the narrow harbour. He had to put the boat back exactly where he found it, rush home, phone the police to report the illegal ocean dumping then jump into bed. Tarkin groaned. It seemed impossible.

Tarkin clenched his fists and drew in deep breaths of air. "Impossible ain't part of your vocabulary, Tark. Remember that. Everything's possible. Everything!" And he shouted it again, "Everything – everything!" as he ran up to the boat and lifted in the winch hook. "So far so good," he yelled. "OK, Tarkin, now back to the ocean!"

He grasped the rope at the helm and swung the boat round. The beach sloped downwards to the sea, which made boat-pulling easy. It flew over the pebbles. In moments the boat nosed into the North Sea with a splash. Yelling, Tarkin jumped in and turned the key to start the engine.

"We're harbour bound!" he shouted, and, Captain once more, tilted the rudder homewards.

Chapter 34

In another ocean, on the tiny island of Sule Skerrie, Magnus Fin felt happiness zip through his strong seal body. Moonlight threaded into the cave and fell upon Miranda. With each passing moment her once shrunken body filled out. Fin watched as the white veils that sat over her eyes drew back, like curtains opening. He stared into the shining green eyes of his grandmother.

Slowly she nodded her head. Then, barely louder than wind in the grass, Fin heard her whisper, *Thank you.*

He wanted to tell her he had found the cause of the sickness. He wanted to let her know that very soon the dump would be cleared up. For all he knew, Tarkin had already called the police. Then the Scottish Environment Protection Agency would come and haul out every dumped fridge, rotting battery and oozing tank. What if Tarkin hadn't phoned yet? Fin needed to be on his way. But still the thought-speech refused to come. Perhaps Miranda understood. Perhaps it didn't need words, not even selkie words. She nodded once more and whispered again, *Thank you.*

Miranda lowered her head back down on her mattress of sponge and kelp. She must have murmured some words in the old tongue to the grey seal, for soon after, the seal said to Magnus Fin, *She will sleep now. The sickness has passed – thanks to you, Fin. Come, your job is done. Come and eat, and rest on the rocks. You have a long journey home.*

Fin looked one last time at his grandmother. She slept peacefully now. He longed to tell her the bay would soon be clean. Beautiful as it was, they wouldn't have to always stay at Sule Skerrie. Soon they could freely roam the seas again and return to the coves and waters close to his home.

For home would not be home if there were no seals in the bay. Who would he play his penny whistle to every morning? Who would sing to him as he spent hours beachcombing or fishing from the rocks? He struggled one last time to form thought-speech.

Getting clean, was all he managed to say after a good deal of concentration.

Miranda's eyes flickered. She looked at him then faintly murmured, *Good, Magnus Fin, that's good.*

Magnus Fin rocked himself out of the dark cave. The brightness of the moonlit night glared after the darkness inside. Blinking, he slithered over the dark rocks and slipped into the sea. A warm feeling coursed through his selkie blood. Round the other side of the island he heard the seals bellowing and splashing in the water. Lifting his nose Fin sniffed the salty air.

He turned his head in the direction of home, looking down the long silver moon path he would travel. He caught a flash of something black dipping in and out along this path. Whatever it was appeared to be swimming at great speed straight towards him.

My great nephew, I believe? The words came from a

handsome, black bull seal. He breached the water in an arc and plunged towards Magnus Fin. *I am Ragnor's uncle. Loren's the name. Now, don't go just when I arrive. You'll need to eat first. Come on, Magnus Fin. I've got fresh haddock. Hungry?*

Normally Fin liked his fish fried, grilled or baked – not raw. But he was a seal now. Normally didn't count. He nodded and plunged down through the water, following his great-uncle, who turned somersaults, honking and yelping. *They are around here somewhere, these haddies,* the large black seal called to Magnus Fin, who bumped up right behind. *We just have to catch them first.* Then he bared his teeth, as though showing Fin how to catch them. *Come on, follow me.*

Fin's great-uncle Loren was a fine hunter. His muscular body darted through the water, slowing for an instant then pushing forward. In a flash he spotted a fish and was after it. In the next flash it was eaten.

Fin followed another haddock, in a half-hearted kind of way. His human thoughts and feelings still guided him. He didn't really want to eat a raw fish, or catch it with his teeth. Loren splashed through the water, caught another haddock and tossed it towards Fin. He'd be offended if Fin didn't eat it, so Fin opened his mouth and nibbled at the fish with his sharp teeth.

Good, eh? said Loren.

Magnus Fin nodded. It was! Then he tore hungrily at the haddock and gulped it down. It tasted much better than he had expected and gave him strength for the long journey back.

He lifted his head above the surface and to his amazement saw a throng of seals surrounding him.

Here are more friends and family, Fin. They are saying thank you and goodbye.

Loren guided Magnus Fin away from Sule Skerrie. Staying close to the island, the other seals, all crooning, yelping and clapping, cheered him on: this *Sliochan Nan Ron* who had brought the medicine for Miranda.

Magnus Fin blew air out through his soft nostrils and fanned out his tail fins. He needed to let Loren know that he and all the other selkies could soon return to the bay. He struggled to form his thoughts. *We'll get the bay clean*, Fin managed to say, *get rid of the sickness – then you can come back*. Loren looked at him. He nodded his head, but whether he believed him or not Fin couldn't tell. The gentle waves lapped around him. Sule Skerrie lay behind him. Far in the distance Cape Wrath beckoned.

That would be a good thing, Loren said, twisting back towards Sule Skerrie. *When the bay is clean we'll set Shuna and the other seals free. Now go, and greetings to Ragnor, and to Aquella, and thank you, Magnus Fin.*

Then Magnus Fin plunged forward. He didn't look back. The deep song of the seals went with him, but even that, as he made fast headway, soon grew silent. He was a seal alone in the wide deep ocean, and he was going home.

Chapter 35

Eastwards he swam: darting, diving, rearing out of the salty water, then plunging deep into the rolling waves. Rafts of gulls, disturbed from their slumbers on the winter's sea, flew up screaming above him. Dolphins and porpoises rocked in his wake. Through the deep swelling waters of the Pentland Firth he cleaved. Over sunken ships he glided. Fin rounded the point at Duncansby Head. In and out of the mighty stacks he weaved, his whole body thrilling as he felt the familiar waters of the North Sea.

Strands of moonlight penetrated the dark water. Rounding a jutting rock Magnus Fin saw, lit up in a watery moonbeam, a familiar and unpleasant sight. He shivered, ready to dive into the kelp forest for cover when suddenly he remembered, he was no longer a skinny child in a wetsuit. He was a powerful seal.

Hello. How are you? Fin called out.

The fish gang huddled together and pushed their ragged leader to the fore. *We ain't doin' no harm. Not us.*

No way. We just – um …

Cruising? said Magnus Fin. *Or loafing around?*

He heard them whimper. He heard their rusting hooks grate against each other as they jostled. *No! Oh no, don't eat us, bro.*

Yeah. We taste bad.
Real bad.
We're just bones.
And scales.
And rustin' hooks.
We're riddled with disease.
Don't eat us, brother.

The fish gang had changed their tune. Magnus Fin swam closer. They looked even more ragged than he remembered. Shreds of plastic bags and cotton buds were twisted up in their hooks.

You look nice, bro.
Yeah, real bonny.
Yeah. No sense getting stomach ache with us.

The fish nodded, all the time slinking away from the big seal with the weird mismatched eyes and dangling necklace. Fin felt sorry for them. He could see how their ribs and bones stuck out. Their eyes bulged. They were dressed in shabby scales, wounds and festers.

Magnus Fin glided closer, swishing his two long tail fins lazily back and forth. *Look,* he said, *I won't eat you. I'm not hungry. Honest! I'm not even a real seal – I mean, not completely.*

The fish gang stared at him and huddled even tighter together. They'd heard all kinds of excuses in their long and difficult lives. *Sure you're not!* they all chorused, the smaller gang members trying very hard to hide behind the bigger ones.

Yeah – you're a goldfish.
Na – he's a lobster!
Na – definitely a whale, dontcha think?

Fin had no time to lose making small talk. He bared

his sharp teeth and in seconds they fled. For ragged old fish, they could move fast when they had to. Fin laughed and plunged onwards.

Magnus Fin turned south and ploughed down the seas. He drew closer to the coast, skirting the steep craggy cliffs. Soon he would arrive in his home waters. He slowed down, excitement surging through him.

While heading up the coast, hours or minutes ago, the great change had happened. Trust, that's what Aquella had said, and that's what he had done. Fin flicked his tail fins through the water, waiting for this mighty seal body to change back into a boy. He lifted his head from the water and looked around. He recognised these cliffs. Far in the dim distance he could see the familiar outline of his house, and further along the coast, the cave. With his keen hearing he could hear music from the village hall. Any moment he would be back in the bay. His eager thoughts turned to panic. He glanced down at his strong round animal form. He was still a seal. Why hadn't he changed?

I trust, he thought. Over and over he repeated the word in his mind, *trust, trust, trust*. But nothing happened. Magnus Fin, swimming into the familiar shallow waters of the bay, was still a seal. And though it had served him well and taken him at great speed the long distance to Sule Skerrie, he longed to be back in his human form.

He had reached the skerries. There, above him, was the black rock. In the cumbersome shape of a seal, Fin didn't know how to heave and haul himself over these craggy rocks of all different shapes and sizes. Jump, run, leap, yes, but not rock on his belly.

Miserably he skirted the mast of the sunken ship and drifted on past the cave. Slowly he swam further up the beach until he came to a small shingle cove. In the shallow water he felt the scrape of sand and shells rub against his seal's belly. Fervently he hoped the change would suddenly happen. But it didn't.

Nothing happened. It was his flippers and not his hands that met the rough shingle of the beach. It was the strong round body of the seal that rocked and heaved itself out of the water, crushing shells under his weight. He tried to rid his mind of the clamouring thoughts that told him he would always be like this – a creature of the sea. Never would he run along the beach. Never would he jump from rock to rock. Never would he play basketball or talk with a human voice.

Lifting his seal head, Magnus Fin could make out, in the distance, the outline of the cave. Where was Tarkin now? And Aquella? And the wild creature in the net? Where were they? The beach was deserted.

Perhaps, Fin thought, he needed to peel himself out of the skin. He squirmed from side to side over the gritty sand. He rubbed his pelt with his flippers. He smacked his tail fins up and down on the shingle. He rolled from side to side. He wriggled. Whimpering now, he rocked himself vigorously back and forth. But try as he might nothing took the seal skin off him. He slumped his head onto the beach, exhausted. He was trapped in this body. A large tear rolled down his soft dog-like head.

I'm sorry about this, M F.

Slowly Fin turned his head. There, inches from his dark soft nose, sat the crab. *I am really sorry. I don't know what do say. You did a great job, M F.*

Through moist eyes Fin stared at the crab. There was nothing to say. For a while the seal and the crab lay on the beach side by side in silence. Then the crab said, *Neptune says thank you. He's busy. Very busy. He's trying to wipe oil from fish's scales and bird's feathers. He's far away. He couldn't come himself. But he wants you to know he is grateful for everything you've done. Maybe that's some consolation for you.*

Still Fin stared at the crab. The crab clicked his nippers together and seemed uncomfortable. *Look, Fin. I'm really sorry about this. I'm just the messenger. Um – nice necklace by the way.*

And with that compliment, the crab scuttled away. Fin lifted his neck and heard his moon-stone scrape against a shell. After all this time it was still there, hanging round his neck. Fin brought a flipper round to touch the lucky stone his father had given him on his eleventh birthday.

Patting the moon-stone, Fin felt warm tears course down his sleek face. He lifted his head and blew through his lips. His deep seal's cry pierced the night.

Chapter 36

Aquella, sensing it was time for Magnus Fin to return, had come to the mouth of the cave. She left Ronan sleeping peacefully by the fire covered in her warm jacket. She looked anxiously out over the moon-dappled water. Where was Magnus Fin? Her keen sight picked out a floating branch and a buoy – but no sign of Fin.

Fin, she called anxiously, *Magnus Fin.* No reply. She called in her thoughts; she called with her voice. Only the crackle of burning wood at her back and the soft breathing of her brother called back.

Aquella ran down to the beach. Tarkin and the boat had gone. She ran further along the beach. Suddenly she stopped in her tracks and lifted her head. A faint cry sounded on the wind. She ran faster now, following that cry, up the beach and over the rocks, away from the cave and the skerries. She ran as fast as she could up the coast, her webbed feet crunching down into the shingle.

"Fin!" she cried, her voice breaking as she ran. "Magnus Fin!"

When she found him he was rolling backwards and forwards, helplessly flapping his flippers against his body.

"Oh, Fin!" she cried out. "Fin! What happened to you?" It was she who had told him to trust the change.

Now he was stuck. She sunk to her knees, reached out and held him. The exhausted seal on the beach now lay still, whimpering. Aquella pressed the side of her face against the sleek fur of her cousin. How long, she wondered, had he lain there, squirming, wriggling and calling for her?

She knew it was Fin. The black hair of the boy was changed into the black sleek fur of the seal. The green and brown eyes were now the eyes of the seal. There was even something about the shape of the face that was his. Changed, but not changed.

Miranda is well, Fin managed to say, each word like a faint rustling. *But we still have to clear the dump.* Perhaps the closeness of Aquella gave strength to Magnus Fin, for his thoughts came, stronger now as he lifted his seal head. *I didn't know how to change*, he said. *Help me, I'm scared. I don't know how to take off the skin.*

Aquella hardly knew either any more. She gazed up at the moon, as though she'd find an answer in that silvery face. She turned to watch the waves curl up the shore. Frantically she swept her fingers through the shingle. Her mind raced now. There were ways. It had happened before. Skins had stuck. Once, a long time ago, she'd helped Ronan. Do it calmly, that's what Miranda had told her, and let the rhythm of your voice mirror the rhythm of the sea.

She closed her eyes and breathed deeply. In her mind she waited for the right song. She breathed in tune with the rhythm of the sea. And as a wave broke and gurgled over the shingle the right song came to her. Like a bright star in a clear night sky it shone.

Fin, she said, drawing up close to her cousin. *Dear*

170

Fin, think of all the good things, think of all the treasures you're going to find washed up on the shore from the Titanic. *Think of that, Magnus Fin. Think of running, walking and jumping over the rocks. Picture your body whole and strong.*

Gently Aquella laid her hands on Fin's sleek head. She said it again, the word she'd said before: *Trust, Fin. Trust.*

Magnus Fin thought of the ceilidh dance and of his mother and father, dancing like waves of the sea. He thought of Christmas and whether he'd get a bike this year, and whether Tarkin's dad would come and visit, all the way from the Yukon. Fin thought of that Ferrari number plate he'd found and did that mean there was a whole Ferrari under the sea, rusting away? He thought of running down the beach path at top speed and leaping over the rocks. He imagined having legs and arms …

Aquella breathed deeply and let the song come.

Sea king
Gull wing
Moon ray
Sea spray
Kith kin
Seal skin
Change

Under her fingers she felt hairs bristle. Hope leapt in her. Again she sang, blending her voice with the ebb and flow of the sea.

Sea King
Gull wing
Moon ray
Sea spray
Kith kin
Seal skin
Change
Change
Change

The bristling under her fingers intensified. She drew back her hand and watched in joy as the seal skin parted, falling away in folds from Fin's shoulders, his chest, his belly. His arms burst out to the side as the strong flippers fell back, like the sleeves of a fur coat when the coat is taken off.

Fin lay quivering on the sand, feeling the warm fur peel away from him. He felt how his soft skin shivered, how out of the bulk that had been his seal's body, his long slim neck arose, and his spine, and bony shoulders. The pads over his strong flippers had gone and small agile hands trembled in their place. Fin stretched these fingers. He ran them through the sand. He shook his head. This time his mop of black hair clung to his face. His long whiskers had gone.

The full roundness that had been the seal seemed to split in two, as though his legs had been glued together and now were wrenched apart. Fin stretched his legs, flexed his webbed feet and wriggled his toes.

He was all there: wiry, thin, human – and dressed in his wetsuit. Magnus Fin lay on the beach in his human form, shaking. Slowly he rolled round and stared up at the moon, then at the round smiling face of Aquella. Now he was laughing. And so was she. By his side lay his crumpled seal skin.

Slowly he sat up, astounded. He gazed down at the skin then up at Aquella. "How did you do that?" he asked, overjoyed that his human speech had been restored to him, along with everything else.

"I sang."

"I can't believe I was a seal. I'm not a full selkie. How did it happen?"

"You are *Sliochan Nan Ron*," she said, "related to the seal folk, and it did happen. Why? Because you've earned it. Look!" Aquella pointed to the very place Fin had lain. The strong round shape of the seal was still imprinted in the sand. "That was you."

Fin shivered. He remembered the crab. The mysterious creature had gone, though his small shape had also left its mark in the sand.

"It's hard to take in, Aquella. It's like a dream." Fin rubbed his legs and patted his arms. "Oh boy – I'm so glad to be a boy!" Then he lifted his hand to his neck. His moon-stone was still there.

Aquella scooped up the seal skin and handed it to her cousin. "Here, Fin, your seal skin. Look after it well."

The warm fur felt both strange and familiar in Magnus Fin's arms. He looked at his cousin then held it towards her. "Here, you have it, Aquella. You're a full selkie. I'm only *Sliochan Nan Ron*. Please – you take it."

Aquella shook her head. "Thanks, Fin, but it doesn't work like that. There is only one for each selkie. No one can wear another person's skin. And I meant it when I said I am happy to be a land selkie. Really – I am. No

Fin – you've earned it. Now you can travel the sea in a wetsuit or a seal skin. It's up to you." She got up and stepped backwards.

Fin lifted the seal skin to his nostrils and breathed it in. He felt his father, his grandmother, even his grandfather, slam into him. Aquella was right; this was his skin. He had earned it.

"So you'll need to hide it somewhere safe," she said. "And maybe you should dry your hair by the fire – and, um, meet your cousin. I mean, your other cousin. Come on!" She ran up the shingle beach, waving for Fin to follow her.

The two of them ran over the sand in the moonlight, Fin with his seal skin flapping in the wind, Aquella with her long black hair flowing beside it.

Never had it felt so good to run with two legs, or to feel the cool night air on his face, or the wind run its fingers through his damp hair. "Wheee!" Fin shouted as they ran along the beach. "I've got arms and legs."

"And you've got a seal skin," Aquella cried.

"The best of both worlds," Fin said, lifting his seal skin up above his head and letting the sleek black pelt flap out like a flag.

Soon they reached the cave. "Wait, Fin," Aquella said, barring the entrance and panting after the run. "We have to be quiet. Ronan is sleeping in here."

Fin, folding his seal skin carefully under his arm, drew up close to Aquella. "Who?"

"Ronan. My brother. You saved him. He's wrapped up in my jacket. I made a bed for him at the back of the cave. I don't want to wake him." She whispered now as she spoke and took Magnus Fin by the hand. "Come and sit by the fire – quietly."

"The thing in the net? The thing that almost killed me in that dump? That's your brother?"

"The dump almost killed him, Fin. Shh! Don't wake him."

They crept in and sat on stones by the fire. Magnus Fin could only dimly make out a figure sleeping under Aquella's puffy jacket. Faintly he heard soft snores coming from the back of the cave.

"That's my brother," Aquella whispered proudly. "It will take a day or so for the poison to leave him. Then he'll go back to the sea. Ronan was always getting into trouble. You know, Fin, he told me he came to find me. He took off his seal skin and ran around looking for me, then was disturbed by dog walkers. There was a fridge dumped on the shore. He jumped in to hide, then the tide washed it away. He can't remember any more. But, poor thing, he shakes and stammers."

"It's the cause of the sickness," said Fin. "I know what it is. And your brother was right in the middle of it. Out there, Aquella, under the sea, it's like a dump. That's where your brother was. It's a wonder he didn't die."

"He must have been better protected from it in his human form," she replied. "Like you, *Sliochan Nan Ron*, you survive all kinds of tricky situations."

The soft snoring of Ronan mingled with the crackle of burning wood. Fin recalled how afraid he had been of Aquella's brother. How his wild staring green eyes had terrified him. How the stink of him had made him feel sick. And now the selkie slept, occasionally making little whimpering noises in his sleep, but for the most part he seemed at peace. Suddenly Magnus Fin remembered someone else who was alive and well.

"Hey, Aquella! Did I tell you?" he said excitedly. "Miranda is well again. The sickness has gone."

"Yes, Fin," she said, firelight glowing in her face, "you told me. Well done, Magnus Fin. You're a selkie prince now."

Chapter 37

Tarkin couldn't believe his luck. Everything was going according to plan. The rudder was easy to tilt and the engine was puttering away bravely. He was approaching the harbour on course, and apart from a little ripple on the sea, conditions were good.

"Right, Tark," he said to himself, bringing the boat level with the mouth of the harbour, "you've got to cut the engine and let her come in slowly. Easy does it. Don't forget the buoys. Don't forget the ropes. Um – what else? Phone the police. What about the anchor? Did Frank drop an anchor in the harbour last night? I can't remember. OK – might as well drop the anchor too. Um – what else? Do I go in backwards or forwards?"

Tarkin was beginning to panic. There was so much to remember. He didn't want to mess up after doing so well. Did it matter which way the boat was facing? The tide hadn't been so far out the night before. Tarkin gasped, seeing, under the orange street lamps that lit up the harbour, how the few boats in the water were tipping over onto their sides. There wasn't enough water to keep them up.

Just then something bumped and threw Tarkin forward. "What's that? Help! Oh, help!" The bottom of the boat was scraping against the stones and sand of the seabed. A black cat meowed at him from a bollard. An owl hooted. And a door in the village hall swung open.

Tarkin had been wrong about the circle of pine trees around the village hall. It was more of a horseshoe than a circle, with a gap to the sea. It was through this gap that Frank was now staring. He'd come out for fresh air. Ceilidh dancing was great fun, but hot work. He was taken by the way the moon lit up the slate roofs and glinted on the sea. And the way an owl landed on a branch and called its deep "tu-whoo!"

Frank wiped his brow and watched the owl fly off, down towards the harbour. Following the flight of the owl, Frank saw his boat. He knew instantly it was his boat. The moon sat on it, illuminating the hull, the stern, and the silhouette of Tarkin, all keeling over to the side.

Something snapped in Frank then. He'd had it with being Mr Nice Guy. He'd had it with trying to bend over backwards to be pleasant to his girlfriend's son. He might have known Tarkin's sudden friendliness concealed some other motive. It also didn't take much looking to work out that the boy and the boat were in trouble.

Frank ran back into the hall. He threaded his way through the dancers, the noise and the music. Keith was trying to teach Martha a quickstep. "I'll not be long. Just going to check on Tarkin."

Then he was off, running down the street and along to the harbour. Frank tore off items of clothing as he ran. A green waistcoat flew through the air. On the harbour wall now he kicked off his shoes. As he ran he judged the depth – too shallow to dive headlong into.

In his tartan trousers and bright yellow shirt Frank ran down the stone harbour steps then jumped into the sea.

After the shock of the freezing water, Frank, gasping, ploughed on. The water came up to his waist. Frank dragged his body through the water, half walking, half swimming. He drew close to his boat. The freezing water took his breath away. He couldn't shout and swim at the same time, so Tarkin was just going to have to get the fright of his life. And, thought Frank, heaving himself towards the keeling boat, it would serve him right.

Tarkin had found an oar. He was just about to lower it to try and free the boat from the shallow water when suddenly the boat rocked wildly. Tarkin was flung forward as the stern of the boat tipped and lurched. In terror he shot a glance over his shoulder – and, Frank was right, Tarkin got the fright of his life. "HELP!" he screamed. "HELP!"

Frank fell into the boat, panting and gasping. The water ran in sheets off him. "What in the name of God," he spluttered, "do you think you're doing?" Frank's eyes blazed. "You've taken me for a mug, Tarkin – and I'm through with it. No one could have done more than I've done."

Tarkin shook his head. He didn't know what to say. Tears rolled down his face. His knees buckled and he sank onto the sloping bench. Frank wasn't done yet.

"I'm here for you!" He planted himself down on the bench opposite. "Can't you see that? I'm here." Frank hit his own chest as he spoke, seawater spraying off him. "I know it ain't easy for you, Tark. Do you think I don't know that? But I ain't Mr Nice Guy no more, get that?"

Tarkin felt his heart fit to burst. Clinging to the side of the tipping boat he nodded. He rubbed his tears with his sleeve. And through it all he felt relieved. The boat wouldn't sink now Frank was here.

"Sorry," he blurted out.

Frank nodded. "So, Tarkin – out for a bit of mermaid spotting?"

Tarkin flashed a look at Frank, but the anger had gone and there was a smile on his face now. Deep down Frank was a good person, Tarkin could see that now, and it was true, this man had bent over backwards to be nice to him.

"I was – on a mission, Frank. Really! I have to call the police. There are loads of poisonous fridges and stuff down in the sea. But the boat's stuck, Frank."

In a flash Frank plunged the oar down and like a gondolier pushed the boat loose of its bed of sand and stones. "Turn the engine now, Tarkin," he shouted.

Tarkin, amazed to be trusted, did as he was told.

Frank took hold of the rudder and in seconds the boat was free and heading out again to the deeper water at the harbour mouth. "At low tide she has to berth further up," Frank shouted, as though he was the sailor and Tarkin his trusty first-mate. "There she goes, that's better. We'll soon have her home. So – sea cleaning, eh, Tarkin?"

"Yeah. Honest, Frank. I winched up a – um, a thing! Magnus Fin needed me, and – um – I needed the boat. There are leaking storage tanks and fridges and freezers and car batteries out there. Honest. Loads. And I have to phone the police."

By this time Frank had secured the boat at the wall of the harbour. He flung a rope round a bollard. "You are one adventurer. Hey, you know your knots, Tark? Run up the steps, buddy. Put two half hitches into that rope and we'll have her moored safe and sound."

Tarkin didn't know his knots. Tarkin didn't like saying he didn't know things. But he wouldn't know two half hitches if they marched up and shook hands with him. He looked at Frank and shook his head. "No. Sorry, Frank. I don't know that one."

"No worries, buddy. I'll show you. Then maybe later you could show me how to dance. Deal?"

Tarkin grinned and nodded his head.

"Glad the throat's better," Frank said as the two of them clambered out of the boat, both of them soaking, and both of them smiling from ear to ear. "Now then – good thing they still have a phone box in this village. Number's 999, buddy. Go on. It's that cute red tardis thing over there. I'll be waiting right here."

Chapter 38

The fire in the cave burned brightly. Shadows danced on the walls.

"A whole hour must have passed since I jumped off the black rock." Magnus Fin was staring out of the cave to the sea. "Look, Aquella – the moon's gone all that way. Mum and Dad are going to get worried. And we have to tell the police about the dump. I need to make a phone call, then get to the ceilidh."

"Ragnor knows where you are, Fin. Don't worry. And he says they're having a great old knees-up at the ceilidh. Soon as we're done, he says, we should get ourselves down there and dance."

Just then a dark shadow flitted across the mouth of the cave. Magnus Fin gasped but Aquella put her hand on his arm. "It's all right, Fin. It's our friend, the winkle picker."

The man stood framed in the entrance, the firelight glowing in his weather-beaten face. "They do their dirty fly-tipping when the moon's bright," he said in a hushed, gravelly voice, "so's they don't have to use headlights. So's no one'll see them. Dirty tippers."

"Where?" Aquella asked.

"They goes through the farm by the old graveyard." Then he was gone, hurrying off with his pail back down to the skerries. A pile of whelks lay on a flat stone at the mouth of the cave.

"They're for Ronan," Aquella said, seeing Fin's look of astonishment. "They're good for him. Do you mind if he borrows your seal skin for a pillow?"

She gathered up the seal skin and the whelks, and went around the fire to the back of the cave. In moments she was back, and ready.

"Well, Fin?" she asked, hands on her hips and her face glowing, "what are you waiting for?"

"Um … the farm beside the old graveyard?"

"That's it. Let's go."

Fin scrambled to his feet. It had been cosy in the cave. It was his father's cave; the place where he had sat and listened to many stories of the sea. But dirty tippers dumping fridges and toxic waste into the sea had never been part of his tales. These people had killed many of his kind and threatened the selkies' very existence. He ran to the mouth of the cave. "Wait for me!"

Aquella was already running up the beach towards the hillside. She ran with bare feet. So did Fin. Their webbed feet pounded down over the grass and over the broken bracken, all brown with autumn. Puffing and panting, they clambered up the heathery hillside sending pheasants squawking and mice scurrying. They knew where the farm was. They knew the old graveyard. What they didn't know was how two children were going to stop the dirty tippers from dumping waste into the sea.

When they reached the farm up by the cliffs they dived in behind prickly whin bushes. "There's folk in the farmhouse," Fin whispered, panting after the climb.

"The curtains are open. I can see them. They're watching TV." The bluish light from a television flickered in the living room.

"They might spot us, Fin. The moon's so bright. We'll have to go the long way round. Come on."

So, instead of dashing straight past the front of the farmhouse, they darted from bush to bush – Aquella, in her new green dress, like a sprite; Magnus Fin, in his wetsuit and mop of black hair, like a sea elf.

"It's not far now," Aquella whispered, with bits of bush in her hair and scratches across her arms. "I can see the gravestones. Hurry, Fin."

Adventures under the sea were one thing. Hanging about in graveyards at night with a full moon looming above was something else. Fin grabbed Aquella by the arm. "Um, Aquella? Look. Do you think this is a good idea? I mean – we're just kids!"

"What do you mean – just kids? Kids are powerful and magical – and anyway, you're half selkie!"

She was right. That was the thing about Aquella. She was always right.

At that moment Fin heard the dim purring of an engine. He glanced down to the sea way below, but there were no boats out that he could see.

"It's the dirty tippers; they're coming down the track," he said. "It's too late to go back. OK, quick, run to the graveyard."

They ran. In moments they reached they old stone wall of the graveyard and clambered over. Fin hunched down behind an ancient crumbling gravestone. Aquella hid behind the marble statue of an angel. Magnus Fin's heart thumped in his chest. To keep in the shadows he pressed his face against the gravestone. His fingers traced the words etched in the stone: DEARLY BELOVED WITH US STILL. 1859. He gulped. He looked down, imagining a skeleton lying just under his feet. The noise of the engine grew louder.

"They're coming," Aquella whispered. "What are we going to do?"

Fin felt goose bumps all over him. "I don't know."

"Think of something, Fin. Quick!"

The dearly-beloved skeleton beneath Fin gave him the idea. "Let's give them the fright of their lives!"

Chapter 39

The lorry reversed down a rutted track. The track skirted the graveyard and came to an abrupt end at the cliff edge where an old fence had been wrenched away. As the lorry neared the cliff it slowed down.

Fin was still pressed up against the old gravestone. The crinkly lichen which grew on the stone dug into Fin's cheek. He shot a glance at the angel. Aquella was crouched down and hiding behind its marble base. They had to act quickly to stop yet more toxic junk being dumped into the sea and getting trapped in the underwater crater. Now Fin could hear the tinny crackling sound of a radio coming from inside the van. He moved to the very edge of his gravestone and peered out. The winkle picker had been right. The dirty tippers were driving without lights on.

Mess your hair up, Fin called. They switched to selkie-speech now. The lorry was hardly a stone's throw away at the other side of the wall. Fin bent down and scooped up a few faded carnations that lay in a jar beside the gravestone. "Sorry skeleton," he whispered, stuffing the flowers into his hair. He heard voices. A door creaked open. The radio crackled low.

"Ye've got three feet. Then we'll get shot o' this lot."

"Dinnae pit me ower the edge mind," the other voice

186

said. "Cos I wudnae pit it past yea."

Fin shot a glance at Aquella. She'd made her hair wild with grass and twigs. She looked like her brother. Fin clutched at his moon-stone. *Right cousin. Let's give them a ghost show.*

He ran his nails up and down the gravestone. A grating noise rose into the air. Aquella did the same, scraping her nails up and down the smooth marble. Then Fin began to moan. Aquella joined in. With her selkie voice she could moan and howl in a pitiful, unearthly way. Then Fin stretched his fingers up above the gravestone and shook them, the way dead man's fingers had waved to him deep under the sea.

Magnus Fin didn't dare peer out. He could hear their choked voices, just feet away:

"What the hell's that?" one of them said.

"Cut it out, Rab."

"You cut it out. I'm doin' nothing."

"I said cut it out or it's you going over the edge. I mean it."

"Oh God! See over that wall! Something's coming out that grave. Look! Oh for God's sake! What the hell's that? Help!"

Fin heard a door bang. He heard a terrified voice cry, "Get out o' here! Oh Mum!"

But Magnus Fin and Aquella weren't finished. *OK, Fin – on with the show!*

They ran from their hiding places and clambered over the wall, wailing like banshees. With their arms waving about they danced in front of the lorry. Aquella, her hair like black fire, green dress twirling, put her hands to her neck and made horrible choking noises. "It's the poison in the tanks," she screeched. "Agh! That's what killed me!"

On cue, Fin jerked up and down in his wetsuit like a frenzied break-dancer, his hair sprouting carnations and his green eye and brown eye staring wildly at the two men who sat shuddering in the front of the lorry, clutching each other. Fin made a great show of retching and choking. "Look spirit," he cried in a high-pitched strangled voice, "our killers." Fin and Aquella pointed towards the two men. "The dirty tippers!"

"Help! Get out o' here. Oh Mum! I'm sorry – for everything I did."

"I never wanted to get mixed up in this sordid stuff. They're going to get us. I told the boss. Didn't I tell him? This was never my idea."

"Just ram your foot down, man. Just go!"

Fin and Aquella leapt back over the graveyard wall and crouched down out of sight. They listened while the men shouted and swore and finally rammed the lorry into gear and took off.

Fin stood up. "After them! Quick, Aquella. We have to find out where all the fridges and stuff are coming from."

They leapt back over the wall and sped after the lorry. The track was rough and pitted with holes. In moments Fin and Aquella caught up with them. Unnoticed, they jumped on the back of the lorry, grabbed hold of a handle and balanced tiptoe on a small metal step.

The drive was more bumpy and juddery than any waltzer at the funfair. "Tarkin would love this," Fin whispered, wondering suddenly where Tarkin was.

But there was no time for wondering. By this time the lorry had left the farm track and joined the road.

188

The lights came on. The radio blared. The men seemed to have stopped arguing. The lorry turned up a narrow winding lane and slowed down.

"Soon as it stops, jump off and hide underneath," Fin said.

But that wasn't necessary. As soon as the lorry stopped, the men jumped out and slammed the doors. One of them threw the keys into a drain then they both ran off. They jumped into an old car, revved it and zoomed away.

Fin and Aquella held on for a while longer then, sure the coast was clear, jumped off their perch.

"Well, well, well," said Fin, gazing up at a huge neon sign above a large metal gate. "Look at this: SAFE SOLUTIONS. YOUR ECO-FRIENDLY DISPOSAL EXPERTS. Jeepers! If that's friendly, I'd hate to meet unfriendly."

On the other side of the barbed-wire fence a few hundred fridges, freezers and battered tanks in all shapes and sizes were piled high. "Taking a few toxic short cuts, I'd say." Aquella couldn't believe her eyes. "How many did you find in that dump in the bay, Fin?"

"Loads." A shiver ran down his spine. "I don't like it here. It gives me the creeps. Let's get out of here."

"Poor Ronan," Aquella said, shaking her head and staring at the mound of junk.

Fin pulled at the sleeve of her dress. "Come on. Let's go."

Magnus Fin and Aquella took the quick way back through a field of sheep. As they ran, flowers and moss and twigs dislodged from their hair. Approaching the village they could hear the sound of a foot-stomping jig coming from the village hall.

"We'll catch the end of it," Aquella said. "It's my first ceilidh. I don't want to miss it. And I've been ready all evening." Her new green dress was now looking a bit dirty in places but Fin didn't want to mention that.

"What about Ronan?"

"He'll be fine. It's sleep he needs. And Davie said he'd keep an eye on him."

"Davie? Who's Davie?" By this time they had reached the cottage by the shore.

Aquella beamed at her cousin as she pulled the last twig out of her hair and opened the front door. "The winkle picker, of course. He's a pal of your dad's."

Fin nodded as he stepped into the house. It made sense that Ragnor would befriend winkle pickers, the hours he had spent down by the shore. And Magnus Fin was still nodding a minute later when he picked up the phone. "Yes, fridges and freezers and tanks full of some kind of toxic waste – honestly – loads and loads of them – all dumped and poisoning the sea."

"Well, now that's reported, you'd better go and put your new kilt on," Aquella said.

"Tarkin already told them. The salvage operation – it's already on its way. Good old Tark." Laughing, Fin kicked his heels and five minutes later appeared with his face scrubbed, hair brushed and kilt on.

Aquella whistled. "Wow! You look just like a Scotsman."

"That's cos I am."

"A selkie Scotsman," she added, winking, "and pretty handsome if you don't mind me saying so."

Magnus Fin grinned, then blushed, then ran for the door. "Come on then, selkie – let's dance!"

Chapter 40

"Take two partners for a Dashing White Sargeant."

Tam, the accordion player, squeezed the red and silver box in and out with gusto and Johnny accompanied him on the fiddle while people looked for partners. Some folks bustled around munching peanuts. Jeanette took off her cardigan because she was too warm and Carol abandoned her high heels because it was much easier to do a Dashing White Sargeant in her stocking soles. Then Mr Sargent laughed and told everyone that this was his special dance and he wanted everyone up on the dance floor and anyone not dancing would get detention.

Martha looked at Frank and shrugged, and Frank looked at Tarkin, and Tarkin shrugged. They all said they were sorry, but they didn't know the steps to the Dashing White Sargeant and maybe they should just sit this one out. But Francis said not at all and didn't they all have to start somewhere, and here was as good a time and a place as any.

Ragnor was the star dancer and Keith said if they just followed Ragnor and did what he did they'd be fine. And Barbara said all you do is go round for eight and back for eight – like this, she said, whizzing round the floor and clicking her heels. She whizzed round so fast her long red hair spun out behind her.

Martha coughed, gulped, then took her son by the hand and said they sure would give it a go, and everyone laughed.

So no one noticed Magnus Fin and Aquella come in. They stood at the back of the hall, lit up by the warm colourful lights. They watched the folk from the village, all dressed in their best clothes, laughing, clapping and tapping their feet. They watched Barbara, in her new black and silver sparkly dress, skip around the room. They even watched in amazement as Tarkin stomped his way round the dance floor with Frank at one side and his mother at the other.

"Oh no," Magnus Fin whispered behind his cupped hand. "Sargent's here. Well, I didn't put this kilt on for nothing. Come on. We can't just stand here."

"Yeah," said Aquella, "let's dance." She was at her first ceilidh – Sargent or no Sargent – and already she felt her body sway in time to the music.

Barbara came running up the dance floor, clapping her hands. "Magnus Fin! Aquella! You're just in time. And don't you both look lovely!" She took them by the hands and pulled them to where everyone was gathering for the dance.

Tam and Johnny were already into the first few bars of the tune but Mr Sargent and his wife needed a partner. "Just a wee minute there, lads," Sargent called out, lifting a hand to halt the musicians. "If anybody has a right to dance this dance, it has to be me." So the music was stopped and Mr Sargent bounded over to Magnus Fin. "Now that's what I like to see," he boomed, "a young man in a kilt. And on St Andrew's day too! My good lady and I need a partner – Magnus

Fin – so, if Magnus Fin would do us the honour, Magnus Fin could dance the Dashing White Sargeant with the Sargents!"

Fin burst out laughing. "Aye, why not?" That left Aquella to dance between her Uncle Ragnor and Aunty Barbara.

And if Ragnor was the star dancer – well, Aquella was the moon itself. She danced like a wave of the sea and her long black hair spun round with every twirl of her lovely green dress. Up the threesomes went hand in hand to meet another threesome, feet drumming the beat. Folk whooped and cheered then under arms they dipped and on to meet the next threesome.

Round for eight they whizzed, and back for eight, and all the time Tam was keeping time, whacking his foot up and down on the wooden floor, his fingers flitting like frenzied things over the keys and the accordion bouncing up and down on his knee. Johnny flashed the fiddle bow like lightning. No one could resist the music.

Tarkin clicked his heels, grinning at Fin and Aquella as they spun round. He could whoop and cheer as loudly as anyone.

"It's great you came along, Tarkin," Frank shouted above the music as the whole company stamped their feet.

Tarkin nodded, "Aye," he shouted. And it was. "Muckle great."

Ragnor, Barbara and Aquella's threesome met the threesome of Mr and Mrs Sargent and Magnus Fin. They moved in and out like waves. In for three, back for three. As they danced, the bright emerald eyes of Ragnor met the eyes of his son. Magnus Fin winked, first with the green eye, then with the brown. One for the land, the other for the sea, and both of them glistening.

How is it, son, asked Ragnor, *under the sea?*

Fine, Dad. Just fine. Or it will be soon.

And Miranda? Tell me, Fin, how is she?

At that moment all arms were lifted high as the music soared. Magnus Fin swung his kilt. Tarkin and Aquella cheered.

Fine, Dad. The sickness has gone. Miranda is well!

And it wasn't long after, when folk were choosing partners for a Strip the Willow, that the sirens sounded. Magnus Fin, Aquella and Tarkin rushed to the window and peered out. Blue lights flashed on the road outside. It was rare in that small village to hear the wail of sirens. Soon everybody had rushed to the windows, craning their necks to see what all the commotion was about. Tarkin was busy explaining to his mother and to Frank, "I told you. We were on a clean-up mission. And I phoned the police. I told them all about it."

Fin flopped down on a seat and sighed with relief. So they *had* taken the phone calls seriously. He felt a great weight fall from his shoulders. Now all he wanted to do was eat a sausage roll and dance.

But everybody made a fuss. Dancing was put on hold while Tarkin told everyone how toxic waste had been dumped in the bay. Fridges, would you believe – and loads of them! Magnus Fin, Aquella and himself had discovered it. Well, Magnus Fin most of all, Tarkin admitted, but he and Aquella had been a great help. And because of it seals were dying. And the Scottish

194

Environment Protection Agency said they'd get things in place and start their clean-up at first light. With their equipment and their highly-trained divers, they hoped to have the salvage operation completed in a day or two.

The music started up again and it was three cheers for Magnus Fin, Aquella and Tarkin – and no one cheered louder than Mr Sargent. That was followed by a rousing rendition of "For They're All Jolly Good Fellows!" and that was followed by piping hot sausage rolls. Fin ate a few then stuffed a few into his sporran. He knew a few hungry hoodlums in the sea who looked like they hadn't had a good meal for years. *Hope you fish like sausage rolls*, Fin thought, beaming from ear to ear while stuffing yet another one into his sporran.

Chapter 41

All through the night, the bay was buzzing with cranking, splashing and whirring noises. But both Magnus Fin's and Tarkin's families were so tired after a night's dancing that they slept through it all. By the time they all woke up that Saturday morning on the first day of December, half the village was lined up along the harbour wall, watching with fascination as the Scottish Environment Protection Agency, with divers wearing full chemical protection gear, salvaged fridge after freezer, after battery, after leaking metal storage tank.

Magnus Fin, though, in the cottage down by the shore, would be happy if he never saw another fridge as long as he lived. While his parents and Aquella ran into the garden after breakfast to observe the big clean-up, Fin sat at the kitchen table and helped himself to more porridge, another dollop of cream and another large drizzling of honey. When he'd licked the bowl clean he took some bread crusts, then ran up to his bedroom and stuffed them into his sporran, which was now swelling like an udder.

He could hear Aquella and his parents cheering outside. "Come on down, Fin," his father shouted.

"Yeah, come on, son," his mother chimed in, waving up to him. "It's great fun. You wouldn't believe how much stuff they're bringing up."

Fin pressed his nose up against his bedroom window and watched. It was like a party out there. With every new item that the deep-water crane forked up and dropped into the toxic-waste disposal vessel, a rousing cheer went up.

"And folk are saying the fat cat bosses of Safe Solutions will go to prison," Ragnor shouted up to Magnus Fin. "So tell us, son, what do you want for Christmas? You can have whatever you want."

Fin opened his window and stuck his head out. "Can I get, um – a mountain bike?" His voice trailed off and he quickly added, "Or a new pair of trainers would be fine." He knew his parents didn't have much money. And now they had Aquella to look after as well. He saw his parents look at each other for a while, considering. Then he saw them smile.

"What colour of bike, Fin?"

"Yippee!" he cheered, so loudly he wondered if it would waken Ronan. *Ronan?* He had forgotten all about Ronan – and about his own new seal skin.

From the garden Aquella caught her cousin's thoughts. She swung round and nodded. Fin dashed downstairs and into the garden.

"Off beachcombing then, son?" Barbara asked. "You never know what you might find with all that junk dislodged."

"I'll come with you, Fin," Aquella said. "Come on, race you to the beach."

They hadn't run far when Magnus Fin stopped and shouted back at the top of his voice, "Red!" Then he turned and sped along the beach path.

As they approached the cave they saw a curling wisp

of blue smoke. "Looks like the fire's still going," Fin said, slowing down. "Do you think that man's still there?"

"You mean Davie?"

No sooner had Aquella spoken his name than the winkle picker stepped out of the cave. "Far too busy out there for me," he said, nodding in the direction of the clean-up operation. Saying nothing more, he picked up his sack of whelks and set off along the beach path.

"Thanks, Davie," Aquella called out after him, "thanks for staying with him. And thanks for everything."

The winkle picker stopped for a moment, looked back at Aquella and Magnus Fin then smiled.

"Bye, Davie," Fin said, waving.

"Bye, Magnus Fin," he said, nodding his head. Then Davie adjusted his sack of whelks on his shoulder and, humming to himself, carried on his way.

Fin hesitated at the mouth of the cave. "Um, maybe you should go in. I'll just wait here." Fin stepped back to let Aquella past.

"No, Fin. I know he's my brother, but he's your cousin. And he's sleeping on your seal skin." She took Fin by the sleeve and tugged him into the warm cave. "Ronan?" she called, hurrying now to the back of the cave, "Ronan?"

She gasped when she saw her brother, then she laughed. She fell to her knees and clasped his hand. "Look at you in my puffy jacket. You look like me."

He did, with his long black hair, his bright green eyes and now with Aquella's puffy pink jacket on. Ronan was sitting up, leaning against the wall, a pile of whelks on one side of him and a tin cup of steaming hot tea on the other.

"Are you feeling better?" Aquella asked, squeezing his hand.

Ronan looked at her, blinked a few times then nodded. He still looked weak but a hundred times better than he had looked the night before. "Look, Ronan." Aquella got to her feet to let Fin come forward. "This is our cousin, Magnus Fin. He is *Sliochan Nan Ron* and you slept on his seal skin."

Ronan lifted his head to stare at his cousin but if he did recognise Magnus Fin he didn't show it. He managed a faint smile. Then his hand moved. Slowly he lifted his arm, free now from barnacles and seaweed. He held up Fin's seal skin.

"Take it, Fin," Aquella urged him. "Go on, he's giving it to you."

Fin stepped forward and took it. "Thanks. Hey, thanks very much, Ronan."

"And now," said Aquella, kneeling beside her brother again, "we'd better try and find out where you left *your* seal skin, Ronan. Can you remember yet?"

Ronan closed his eyes and appeared to concentrate. "He thinks it's in here somewhere," Aquella said to Fin, "but I've searched everywhere and I can't find it." Just then Ronan's eyes flashed and he seemed excited. "Where is it, Ronan? Where's your seal skin?"

Ronan tilted his head and gazed up at the ceiling. With his free hand he pointed to a high ledge. "Away up there?" Aquella gasped. "Are you sure?"

Ronan nodded. He tried to stagger to his feet but fell back. "It's OK, Ronan. Your strength will come back. But now you have to take it easy." She looked up at Magnus Fin. "Um – Fin?"

Magnus Fin knew what was coming. He looked up at the high ledge. "You want me to climb up there?" She nodded. "Right to the top?" She nodded again. So did Ronan. Fin groaned. "It's really high."

"But it's got foot ledges. You'll manage. I know you will. Please, Fin?"

It *was* high. Some of the foot ledges were hardly two inches thick. Fin, though, had had a lot of practice on the school climbing frame, so scaling the cave wall wasn't half as hard as he thought it might be. He had almost reached the high dusty ledge when a bat, disturbed from its daytime slumbers, brushed Fin's hair then flew out of the cave.

"Wow!" Fin called out, gripping the ledge, and with his free hand feeling along the rocky shelf. "Bat attack! Hey! I can feel a seal skin. It's been a bat's bed!"

"Throw it down, Fin."

He did, wondering as it fell what the bat was going to do for a bed now. He didn't wonder for long. "Hey, Aquella!" he shouted down. "Throw my seal skin up here. It's a good hiding place. No one will ever find it here." *Except a bat that is*, he thought, grinning. Magnus Fin liked bats. He liked the idea of a bat using his seal skin for a bed. And his seal skin would feel safe in his father's cave.

By the time Fin was down, Ronan was asleep again, this time with his own seal skin as a blanket, and Aquella was tending to the fire.

"When will he go back to the sea?" Fin asked.

"When the sea is clean, and when he's better. Tonight maybe?" Aquella put some wood on the fire then stood up. "You know, Fin, when I was on the beach last night,

I'm sure I saw a lot of pottery bits and blue sand glass, and – I'm pretty sure I saw a shark's tooth." By this time she was at the mouth of the cave. "Race you down to the tideline!"

And she was gone, her bare feet gliding over the sand, her long black hair flapping in the wind. Fin glanced back at Ronan, then up at the high shelf where his seal skin was hidden. The fire crackled – and for a fleeting moment he remembered words from an old story his father used to tell him in this very cave …

Once upon a time, there lived a beautiful seal… Her eyes, folk said, were human eyes. So beautiful was she that many tried to hunt her. But they never could. She was known as the bright one …

Then Magnus Fin ran from the cave, feeling a wave of joy and happiness ripple through him. "Hey! Wait for me!"

Chapter 42

That Sunday morning Magnus Fin woke early. It was still dark outside. The clunking and banging noises that had gone on all day yesterday and late into the evening had stopped now. Every fridge and freezer and all the other junk had been lifted. The only sounds in the cottage that early December morning were the crashing of the waves as they broke over the pebbles and the low hum of the boiler.

Lying in his boat-bed, listening to the swish and roll of the waves outside, Fin felt himself nod back to sleep. Dreamily he thought of Ronan and how he had slipped into the sea late last night, yelping happily. Fin rubbed his eyes. Wouldn't it be lovely to stay in his warm bed and go lazily over and over in his head everything that had happened since finding the writing on the rocks? But he had an appointment.

Magnus Fin swung his legs over the side of his bed, hearing the soft padding sounds of Aquella in her attic room above. Fin got dressed in the dark, fumbling for his old trainers and his jeans and fleecy top. He patted his moon-stone that hung around his neck and shook his hair, which was now so long it was forever flopping in his eyes. Tarkin said he should gel it and spike it up, maybe even dye it pink! Fin ran his fingers through his hair, by way of combing, and wondered if Tarkin was up yet.

He opened his top drawer, pulled his penny whistle out of a sock and stuck it in his jeans pocket. He heard Aquella tiptoe down the stairs. "Psst!" she called, tapping softly at his bedroom door. "Magnus Fin, are you up?"

"Course I'm up." He opened his door an inch and peeped through the gap with his green eye. "I've been up for ages." They spoke in whispers. This was Sunday morning. Ragnor and Barbara always had a long lie on a Sunday morning.

"Do you want jam or cheese?" she asked.

Fin thought for a second. "Both."

By the time Magnus Fin and Aquella had made and packed their breakfast picnic, the first glimmers of colour were seeping over the rim of the sea.

"Do you think Tarkin will come?" Aquella asked as she closed the cottage door and they stepped out into the chill of the early morning.

"Course Tarkin will come. Knowing Tarkin, he's probably there already."

They set off along the beach path, singing as they went. They hadn't gone far when the flash, flash from a torch blinked out of the half-darkness.

"See! What did I tell you? Good old Tarkin." Fin sped off across the sand and on to the skerries. Aquella ran behind, awkwardly on account of the welly boots Fin insisted she wear.

Then it was high-fives on the rocks. "I've been here ages, man. I got hot chocolate and something called tablet, and peanut butter on a bagel." Tarkin grinned and thumped Fin on the back. "Mission accomplished, dontcha think?"

Fin smiled and nodded, glancing first at Tarkin, then at Aquella, then out to sea. The salvage operation was complete and the Environment Protection vessels had gone. All was still out at sea. Fin saluted. "Aye, aye, Captain – mission accomplished!"

Tarkin turned round to a flat ledge behind him and spread out their breakfast as if it were a table. "And you said they like music, so I brought my guitar."

"Wow, Tarkin! You look like you've moved in!" Fin laughed and perched on the black rock beside him, noticing, with the help of Tarkin's torch, that there were no M Fs to be seen. The writing on the rocks had well and truly gone – washed away by the tide.

The three of them ate their breakfast picnic perched high on the black rock. They munched noisily, watching the eastern sky turn from a pale green to a deep red.

"What a show!" said Tarkin, his cheeks full with tablet. "Oh man, this is awesome, and to think I sleep through it every morning."

"If we're lucky we might get a bit of sound to go with the colour," Aquella said, licking a crumb of tablet from her lips.

Magnus Fin spotted them first. Tarkin was tuning his guitar. Aquella was going for her fifth piece of tablet. Fin was scanning the ocean. As he watched, a sleek black head lifted slowly from the water. The dark kind eyes of a seal looked straight at him. Fin gasped. Then another seal lifted its head from the water. The sea was glittering now as the sun rose and more and more seals broke the surface.

"Stand up," Fin whispered, his voice choked with emotion, "Tarkin, Aquella, quick! Stand up. They're here!"

The three children rose hurriedly to their feet, all of them balanced on the high black rock. Tarkin strummed his guitar. Magnus Fin whipped out his penny whistle and played his tune. Aquella sang. The clear and sparkling sea lapped gently against the rocks as fifty or more seals lifted their shining heads out of the water and sang back.

As Fin played he felt his heart fit to burst. In the throng of singing seals he could see Ronan, and beside him Shuna. Next to Shuna, big, black and handsome, if Magnus Fin was not mistaken, was his great-uncle Loren.

Fin stopped playing and waved at the seals. He laughed then looked up and gasped. Right in front of him, lifting her silvery head from the shimmering water and gazing at him with her shining eyes, was his grandmother Miranda, the bright one of the sea.

Janis Mackay

Author Interview

Q. How did you become an author?
Janis Mackay [JM]: I've always liked writing. I have written poems and short stories and had them published, but I suppose being an author means having a book published. *Magnus Fin and the Ocean Quest* is the fourth book I wrote for children – but the first to be published. So I suppose winning the 2009 Kelpies Prize made me an author!

Q. What inspired you to write Magnus Fin and the Moonlight Mission*?*
JM: I live by the sea. I was walking along the beach and saw a few dead seals. I also saw a lot of rubbish. And I felt so sorry for those innocent and lovely creatures who live so close to us and have to suffer because of our rubbish.

Q. Who is your favourite character from the Magnus Fin books?
JM: At first I think Tarkin was my favourite. He is very free and unusual and quirky and I like that. Then Miranda was my favourite in a mystical selkie way. But I have to say Magnus Fin. He is a bit shy but he is also

brave. He is sensitive and cares about animals – and he wants to enjoy his life and make a difference, not hurt people.

Q. How long did it take to write Magnus Fin and the Moonlight Mission?
JM: Quite a long time. I wrote the book, then re-wrote it, then wrote it again, then edited it, then edited it again. Probably a year in all.

Q. How do you decide what the cover of your book looks like?
JM: I think Nicola Robinson (the illustrator) is wonderful. I love her covers. I like the covers to be stories in themselves – so by looking at the cover you get a real sense of what the story will be like. For this cover I thought it would be good to have a seal, and Magnus Fin in the whirlpool.

Q. The Magnus Fin books are full of cool sea creatures. Which one is your favourite?
JM: Of course I love seals. I live close to them and have seen them on the beach as pups. I have looked into their eyes and heard them sing. I watch them swim.

Q. Magnus Fin's friend Tarkin can't swim. Is there anything that you can't already do that you'd like to learn?
JM: I'd like to sing well, cook a good meal, climb mountains, and speak fluent French. There are lots of things I can't do, but I also know it takes a lot of practice to do certain things – like play the piano for instance. Mostly I want to write really well, and that I suppose is what I practise most.

Q. What is the best thing about being an author?
JM: There are lots of wonderful things. One is creating characters who come alive. Although I spend most of the day on my own writing, I feel I am in great company. Another wonderful thing is meeting children for whom Magnus Fin and the gang are real.

Q. Do you plan your stories in advance?
JM: When I first began writing I didn't know what the next sentence would be until I wrote it nor did I know what was going to happen next. I think that is a good way to write, especially when you are just beginning. I plan a little bit now and try to strike a creative balance between planning and being spontaneous. Writing is an amazing thing. You can plan clever things, then somehow as you write, the story tells you to do something else. That is why writing is exciting.

Q. Magnus Fin is half selkie. If you could be any supernatural creature, what would you be?
JM: An angel!